The Long Road Back

A Novella
by

John McGrath

Author's Note

Releasing this book out into the world (a story that lived, for ten years, solely inside my own head) is the scariest thing I've ever done. Because it is yours now. It is entirely up to you what you think of my story. I can't make you like it and I certainly can't stop you from giving it 1 out of 5 stars. But that's the reason I love writing so much.

I find it incredible that a person can read a passage and feel... happy, sad, lonely, empowered, passionate, inspired. All from a combination of 26 simple letters on an otherwise blank page.

I don't expect the Earth to move for you when you read this book. The stars will not align and it won't change your life. All I can say is this:

I enjoyed writing this story. And I hope you enjoy reading it.

For Ann Marie, who built
the fire,
and for Jess,
who showed me
how to light it

Chapter One

The sun hung high in the sky the day Teddy awoke in the dream. For it was undeniably a dream, he surmised, after several hours wandering and wondering, piecing together the stubbornly hazy fragments of his memory. Thinking back to the drowsy moments after waking, he was surprised to find that he had no memory of ever going to sleep. Teddy's last memory, as far as he could recall, was one of pacing his office, head facing down towards the bruised and battered rug that suited the room in neither size or style, and setting himself down on the frayed, yet loyal, cotton polyester sofa in the curved corner of his cramped workspace. There was a knock at the door.

Or perhaps there wasn't, he now countered, mistrusting his own senses more and more by the second. This was his most recent memory and even that felt like a lifetime ago. All Teddy could be sure of now was that he most certainly was not in his office any longer. Not mentally present at any rate.

It had been anything between fifteen minutes and two or three hours since Teddy had came to atop a soft bed of sand, blinked dumbly, and rubbed his eyes in bewilderment. The blinding sun reflected off the dull orange landscape that stretched in all directions as far as Teddy's mystified eyes could see. Everywhere was a blanket of sand. There seemed to be nothing upon the arid plain other than beige rocks, sparse whispers of foliage, and a sliver of a path that repelled the sand and pulled itself all the way to meet the horizon. A pale haze hovered above the ground, a relentless pulse of evaporation, as if the sun was melting the vast floor away one inch at a time. There was not a single cloud in the sky, just the burning jewel amidst a deep sea of blue.

"Hello?" Teddy said.

Drawn to the road mere metres away, he stepped unsurely onto the firm tarmac surface and followed the path with his eyes into the distance, before turning and looking the opposite direction.

"What the hell..." he muttered.

He stared questioningly into the sand. The sand stared blankly back at him.

The eerie silence unnerved him. The only sound came from his shuffling feet as he moved gingerly onto the sand for several paces before stopping abruptly and turning to look back at the road. Without fully understanding his own reason, he quickly returned to the path. He seemed to feel, at the very least, less uneasy when his feet were on the road.

"HELLO?" he yelled.

Not even his echo answered him.

After several minutes he realised he could hear the rhythmic beating of his own heart. Further unsettled, Teddy began to walk along the road. Why he had picked this direction he could not say. Again, it just seemed to feel less... less wrong. The movement had a calming effect on his nerves. Of this Teddy was sure. It was the reason he paced in his office. It was also the most rudimentary advice he gave to his patients when they experienced the crippling doubts of indecision: "Walk it off, get the negative ions flowing," he would say cheerfully.

Upon reflection, it was no wonder his office rug was in such terrible shape.

*

Lesley Harper had stirred in the shade. The comfort offered by the sand led her to believe she had woken up in her own bed and it was only when she attempted to turn her bedside alarm clock off and her hand landed on the rough surface of a nearby rock that she realised something was amiss. She let out a quiet yelp of pain and her eyes snapped open. It seemed as if the cluster of rocks perched next to her, each rock as big as her head, was about to tumble on top of her. She quickly scrambled to safety only to be met with the eye-watering brightness of the bare environment.

Lesley gasped in shock. Her bottom lip quivered with fear. She whipped her head round to look at her surroundings. Nothing. Nothing but sand and rocks. Her first thought was a panicked: "I've been kidnapped!"

But there was nobody else around for what seemed like miles.

"I've been kidnapped and dumped here!"

But her clothes all seemed to be in perfect shape, nothing out of place, and she had no injuries of any kind, other than a lightly bruised palm from slapping a rock twenty seconds earlier. In fact, it seemed as if she had simply appeared here, like landing in the middle of a dream.

Lesley paused. She turned to look at the rocks that had threatened to avalanche on top of her. They were perfectly still. All they did was provide shade from the beating sun. Lesley turned again, her mouth agape.

"Er... h-hello?" she asked timidly.

Her words dissipated into the silence.

She could feel her heartbeat thumping in her chest. Her breathing quickened and her teeth chattered.

"Hello?" she begged.

Lesley sank to her knees and sobbed quietly. Where am I? she thought to herself. How did I get here? The last thing I remember is... What? What is the last thing I remember?

Lesley cast her mind back to what seemed like weeks ago.

There was a dull thud and a small smash. Lesley groaned. She had knocked the picture of her parents off of her desk. She rested her head in her hands and sighed miserably. That was her favourite picture. It wasn't even supposed to be in her study. It usually took pride of place on the fireplace in her living room, but one of the workers had left an old dust sheet there and she wasn't sure whether she should remove it – it wasn't hers after all.

This was the last thing Lesley could recall. She had resolved to clean up the mess and then... nothing. After that, she woke up in the sand.

No, she thought. I'm missing something obvious.
Maybe I've blocked it out.
Her train of thought was interrupted, however, as,
through soft tears, she saw a figure in the distance,
walking slowly towards her.

*

Teddy had been walking, lost in confusion and
mismatched memories, for half an hour. He walked
without purpose, turning occasionally and scratching
his head in disbelief, but maintaining a sure footing
on the road, which had gradually widened until it
was several metres across. The landscape barely
changed the further he travelled. There seemed to be
slightly more clumps of greenery and clusters of
rocks. Some of the rock piles, at either side of the
road, seemed large enough to provide some decent
shade from the sun, which still hung ominously in
the sky like a bored spectator to Teddy's lonely
adventure.
There was a whisper behind him and he snapped his
head around. Nothing moved and no sound met his
ears. Resolving that the noise was nothing more than
tumbling sand, he turned away and continued
walking.

Beads of sweat started to slowly slide down his forehead and he reached up his arm to wipe the perspiration on his sleeve. His eyes were fixed on a rocky outcrop further ahead where he planned to stop, aiming for respite from the heat.

There were worried thoughts gnawing away at Teddy. He tried to push them from his mind but they always clawed their way back. What's going on? Will I starve? Suffocate? Will I wake up? All he could be sure of was that he felt better whilst he walked along the road. Maybe it was psychological.

Of course it's psychological, he told himself. It's giving me a goal to aim towards, a path to follow. And I'm not going to stop moving because then the doubts will creep back.

He looked up at the sun. It was taunting him.

"Well, I'm not going to stop for long," he grumbled. He lowered his head and looked down at his feet. Maybe it was the heat, or the totally alien surroundings, but he could not process his thoughts properly as he attempted to contemplate theories he had. Other than the determined voice within him that shouted: "It's just a dream!" his mind simply drew a blank every time he considered the alternatives.

Apart from the dark thought that had struck him almost as soon as he woke up. Teddy tried not to dwell on this unpleasant idea and raised his head to look once more into the blank distance.

He stopped in his tracks.

Up ahead, just to the edge of the road, there was a figure hunched over, possibly on its knees.

Teddy hesitantly took a step forward. The figure looked up. It was a woman.

The two locked eyes. Neither of them moved, Teddy taut with trepidation, Lesley frozen with fear.

Teddy's eyes darted to either side, looking for anyone else he should be wary of. Lesley did not break her gaze but was shaken to her core. This must be her kidnapper. And there were surely others she should be wary of.

A full minute passed and Teddy and Lesley remained motionless. Finally, perhaps realising that they were both as uncertain and afraid as one another, Teddy spoke.

"Hello."

Lesley looked around. There was nobody else. There was nowhere for anyone to hide anyway.

"Hi," she replied tonelessly.

There was another long silence.

"What, um... What are you doing here?" Teddy asked.

Lesley raised her hands in a gesture of confusion and innocence.

"I... I don't know," she said.

"Did..." Lesley began after another silence. She looked at Teddy and tried to insert some steel into her voice. "Did you kidnap me?"

Teddy's eyes widened in horror and his mouth fell open. "Wha--" he spluttered. "No, I, God, I swear--"

Lesley realised the truth immediately from Teddy's reaction. "Oh my god, I'm sorry! I just, I thought... I'm so, so sorry, I didn't mean... it," she finished lamely.

In an instant the tension was released. Teddy exhaled in relief then, in spite of the situation, let out a quick laugh. Lesley smiled weakly. She stood up and hastily brushed the sand off herself. Teddy cleared his throat.

"I, er... I just woke up here, further down that way," he said, pointing the way he came. "I don't know what's going on or how I got here. I just, I don't know. I just appeared."

He walked forward as he spoke. "I'm... My name's Teddy."

Lesley stared at him.

"It's short for Edward," he said sheepishly.

She smiled. "I'm Lesley."

They both looked around, far into the distance and then back to each other.

"So," began Teddy. "Any idea what the hell's going on?"

Lesley shrugged.

"I was just about to ask you the same question."

*

Wes was experiencing a surreal sense of déjà vu. He had woken from vivid dreams of sandy wastelands and colourless deserts to a very real depiction of both. In his dream he stood alone on a thin strip of road stretching beyond the limits of his own imagination. Behind him the sky pulsed, a drowning sea of blue, and up ahead, clinging to the horizon, it burst into a deep, thick purple. Clouds meandered lazily along the canvas above, expanding and contracting in a vibrant exhibition of art and artifice. Wes watched, engulfed in the shades of luminescent vivacity, as a harsh wind blew into his path. He threw his hands over his over his face and, when he lowered them, the land and sky were barren. Everything was dead.

The silence woke him.

Wes rolled over on the hard surface and opened his eyes, squinting into the sunlight. He was lying on a wide, rough road that had no markings or personality. On either side lay an endless sea of sand. When he was on his feet, he studied his surroundings. There were a few sterile bushes, sparsely placed apart, and a couple of dead trees, their wood rotted to the core.

Wes stretched and ran a hand through his blonde hair, looking searchingly up and down the road. He stood still for a long time, trying to remember something, anything, that would help him piece together an explanation for where he was. Memories of his seemingly prophetic dream swam to the surface and intertwined with what he was sure was his last real recollection.

He had visited his mother's house in Kansas. He was sure of that. He remembered standing on her porch, searching for the spare key that was usually always hidden under the green garden gnome with the fishing rod. But afterwards...

He rubbed his temples in frustration. "Amnesia," he muttered.

His eyes combed the area again. He did not recognise this place, not even from old army drills from his training. Sure, he thought, they could 'kidnap' new recruits and drop them in the middle of nowhere to fend for themselves. But he was four years out of boot camp. Even the US Army wouldn't bother with a stunt like this.

Wes cleared his throat. "Hey! Hello? Anyone here?" When there was no reply he considered his options. Maybe it was instinct, or perhaps the memory of the dream he had woken up from, but he decided the best course of action was to begin walking down the road in the direction that appeared to contain a little more foliage and possibly a few more signs of life. This thought was still fresh on his mind as he took his first confident steps on his unsure journey.

That was when he saw the body.

It appeared to be no more than a bump in the road from a distance but, as Wes came closer, the unmistakeable figure of a human was evident. He studied the figure from about ten metres away. It was a man - mid-twenties, brown hair, tightly-trimmed stubble. He was sprawled spread-eagled, limp and lifeless, in the middle of the road, his face pointing directly upwards. After hastily glancing around himself, Wes approached the man with his pulse quickening. He thought he saw the man's chest rising a fraction and paused. Concluding that his eyes must be playing tricks, he leaned over the body. Wes checked for any obvious injuries. There were no marks on the man's body so he moved in closer to the face. He was silent while he listened for any breathing. His ear hovered inches above the man's nose.

"Oi, mate. You're blocking the sun."

Wes recoiled in alarm and fell backwards. The man turned his head and looked at him with brilliant blue eyes. They both stared at each other for several seconds. Then the man laughed.

"Who are you, then?" he asked.

Wes gazed blankly back.

"Do you own this place?" the man said, sitting up and gesturing to the sand. "Is this your private beach?"

"What the hell..." said Wes. "What the hell are you doing lying in the middle of the road?"

The man laughed again. "Well, I didn't hear any cars coming."

He watched Wes with a smile on his face. Then he jumped up and offered his hand.

"Sorry about the fright," he said. "I heard you coming and spotted you out the corner of my eye. I just couldn't resist."

He spoke with an English accent and his words came out so quickly that Wes had to focus to understand. Wes took his hand and the man hauled him to his feet.

"I'm Jack," he said, keeping hold of Wes's hand and shaking it. "But you probably knew that, right?"

Wes shook his head. "Ah, no, sorry."

Jack raised his eyebrows in surprise.

"I'm Wes."

"Wes? Cool," Jack said, shrugging off his surprise. "You American?"

"Yeah, Kansas originally. I'm a bit all over at the moment."

There was a moment of awkward silence. Wes looked off to the side. He hated small talk. But still, "Um, you're from England?"

"Yep, up north, that's me. I've never been to America," he laughed.

Wes smiled politely. Why is this man persisting with pleasantries when I don't have a clue what's going on? he thought. He was clearly being set up in some frustrating prank. He hated pranks.

Jack looked around with his hands on his hips. "It's almost exactly how I pictured it."

He turned to face Wes. The American bore a confused expression.

"So," began Jack. "D'you mind telling me where I am? I, er, I can't actually remember how I got here. I just woke up over there," her pointed a thumb over his shoulder, "and, well, I wasn't really sure what was going on so I just... just lay down for a bit."

Wes stared at him incredulously.

Jack smiled weakly. "Of course, it's not the first time I've woke up in the middle of nowhere, but I dunno how I made it to America. In fact... I wouldn't have been drinking or anything..."

He trailed off and looked at Wes for answers. Wes stared at Jack for answers.

"Are you telling me," asked Wes, "that you just woke up here, in this place, and you have no idea how you got here?"

Jack held his hands up. "Guilty."

"Then why are you acting like it's all a big game?" Wes asked, his frustration bubbling up.

"I don't know," said Jack. "I just assumed that someone would come along who knew the place and I'd just, you know, ask them."

"Wha-- This isn't America, Jack. I don't know where I am. I'm totally lost and I don't know what's going on."

He watched as Jack's eyes widened. At least he's taking it seriously now, he thought.

"How long have you been here?" Wes asked.

"T-twenty minutes, maybe, maybe more."

"Okay, okay, okay."

Wes looked into the distance, in the direction he had originally been aiming for. There seemed to be an intriguing invitation offered by the horizon. He felt compelled to travel that way.

"Right, we need a plan," he said.

Jack covered his face with his hands. Wes saw this and resolved that he should be the one to take charge.

"I think we should head down that way. If there's something – or someone – here then I reckon it's down there. We should stick to the road - it runs straight for as far as I've seen... so far. It's pretty hot so we'll take it easy."

Wes clapped his hands together. "Let me know if you need to take a break from mar—er, walking. Maybe you feel you want to squeeze some more sunbathing in?"

He looked at Jack for some response to his joke, but Jack did not seem to have noticed. He had removed his hands and seemed entirely free from stress.

"Does that sound like a plan?" Wes asked.

Jack shrugged. "Sure," he said.

"Or, you know, maybe you've got a plan of your own?"

Jack nodded.

Wes was taken aback. "What, really?"

Jack nodded again.

"Okay, let's hear it, chief."

The Englishman smiled at Wes. "I think we should wait here for other people to come and we can ask them what's going on."

"Are you kidding me?" Wes said. "No-one else is here. Yeah, sure, you were lucky that I turned up but we need to move. No-one's else is turning up. There's no-one else to ask."

"Oh, well, I'm not sure about that," Jack smiled. "In fact, why don't we ask them?"

He nodded over Wes's shoulder. Wes followed his gaze and they both watched as two people walked towards them, partially shrouded by the heat haze rising lazily from the ground.

*

"...and I just can't see this being anything other than some kind of bizarre projection of my own mind," Teddy was saying. "Which means none of this is real, not even you. Uh, I-I mean, I don't mean it like that, sorry..."

Lesley chuckled. "It's okay, I know what you mean. From your perspective then I'm obviously not definitely 'real.' I could be part of a dream you're having, sure. It's possible. But the same can be true for me as well. This could be my dream and *you're* the projection. I know I'm real... I *think*. But that's all I can be sure of. Or not sure of, I guess..."

She looked up at the empty sky. It had been no more than ten minutes since they had met and started walking. The scenery had changed ever so slightly; there was more evidence of nature in amongst the sandy ground, from the abandoned logs sprawled haphazardly on the desert floor to the – admittedly decrepit – bushes that had begun to spring up near the road.

"Of course," said Lesley. "There is the possibility that this all *is* a dream but not just *yours*. And also not just *mine*."

Teddy listened attentively.

"Well," she continued. "What if this is a dream we're *both* having? And we're *both* real?"

Teddy nodded slowly. Lesley paused before going on.

"I can't really explain it. To be honest, I can't really get my head round it myself."

"I think I know what you're getting at," said Teddy. "It's like we're both experiencing the same dream, probably at the same time."

Lesley murmured in agreement.

"The only analogy I can think of for all of this is... It's like we're both plugged into some virtual reality machine at the same time, and we experience things in our own way because it's our current projection of reality. I don't know if that makes sense? Hell, it barely makes sense to me..."

He cleared his throat and scratched his chin thoughtfully. There was that thought that had been troubling him.

"Or..." he voiced slowly. "There's possibly a more unpleasant theor--"

"Look!" hissed Lesley, pointing ahead.

Teddy looked up. In the middle of the road directly ahead of them were two men, one with his back to them, standing perfectly upright, and the other facing them with his hands on his hips.

Teddy and Lesley slowed their pace but kept moving forward. The men turned to look at them. The taller one had a slightly hardened look, but he did not look overtly threatening. If anything, the other man looked bored.

"Looks like there's more than two of us dreaming," whispered Lesley.

They stopped walking and stood warily a few metres away from the men. Nobody moved.

Eventually, Teddy coughed once into his hand.

"Excuse me. Hi there," he said. "Er, this might sound a bit, er, ridiculous, but we, um..."

He glanced sideways at Lesley whose eyes darted from side to side then down to her feet.

"Do either of you know where we are?" Teddy continued. "We're totally lost and can't remember where we, er, parked our car."

Lesley looked at him squarely. Wes and Jack started.

"You know where we are?" exclaimed Wes. "I mean, you know vaguely where we are?"

Teddy's brow furrowed in confusion.

"Yeah, man," said Jack. "Because we have no idea what's going on here, ha! I mean, I just--"

"Woke up?" interjected Lesley.

Jack stopped, his mouth wide open. "Yes," he said slowly. "Just over there. How did... How did you know that?"

Teddy groaned and placed both his hands on top of his head.

"It's obvious, isn't it?" he said. "We, all four of us, have woken up in some desert with absolutely no recollection of how we got here. And I, for one, was really hoping the two of you could shed some light on the situation."

Wes and Jack glanced at each other then stared at Teddy and shrugged apologetically.

"So... you don't really have a car?" asked Jack sadly.

A weak breeze blew across the plain, lightly shaking the nearby bushes and spraying sand gently onto the road.

Chapter Two

Teddy had taken advantage of the shade offered by the nearby rocks and massaged his temples wearily. He sat with his back leaning against the smooth surface and closed his eyes, keen to avoid observing the colourless landscape for too long. Wes stared gloomily into the distance. Jack was lying on the ground again.

It had been a tense few minutes after their impromptu introduction, highlighted with a formal uncertainty and hesitant wariness. Before long, however, it became clear that nobody knew what was happening – a fact that, originally, nobody knew.

"So," said Lesley, pacing from one edge of the road to the other. "Nobody knows what's happening?"

Wes heaved a large sigh. "No," he said. "We've already discussed this. It was literally the first thing we said."

"I know," snapped Lesley. "But I just want to start from the absolute beginning. We must've left something out, or-- Or one of us knows something but we've forgotten--"

"We've all forgotten!" Jack blurted out. "That's why we're bloody lost!"

"Okay, settle down, Jack," hushed Teddy. "Let's think about this logically. We'll piece together what we can and go from there."

"Fine," replied Jack, sitting up. "Sorry, Lesley, was it? Yeah, Lesley, sorry, please continue."

She stared at Jack, momentarily repulsed by his graceless manner, and then cleared her throat.

"Thank you, Jack," she said before turning away from him. "Teddy and I had briefly mentioned the possibility that this is all a dream of some kind."

"How can it be a dream?" asked Wes. "I mean, this all feels real. I'm conscious right now. Besides, how can all four of us be here chatting?"

Teddy answered him. "Well, dreams feel real until we wake up. The question is: what if we're dreaming but we never even went to sleep?"

There was silence for a moment.

"Wh-- Like, what does that even mean?" Wes asked incredulously.

"It doesn't matter. He's just thinking out loud," said Lesley, anxious to get the conversation back on track. "Maybe it would help to share what the last thing we remember is?"

Wes shrugged. "I was visiting my mother's house," he said. "I was standing on the porch, and I remember looking for the key for the front door and... I dunno, that's it. Maybe I found the key, maybe I let myself in, I can't remember."

He scratched his chin and looked at Lesley. Her gaze was fixed on him and she was nodding intently. She was listening attentively but it seemed to Wes that she was perhaps trying a little too hard to look interested. Some people like to be in charge, he thought. And they're not always the people best suited to the position. It takes far more to be a proper commander.

Lesley turned to Jack. "What about you," she asked. "What's the last thing you remember before waking up here?"

Jack picked himself up lazily. He stretched and ran both hands deliberately and delicately through his hazelnut hair.

"Let's see," he said at last. "I was on my way home. I usually walk, it's safe enough for me because all the people like me, you know?"

He looked expectantly at the other three but was met with blank faces.

"I was on my way home from football training," he explained patiently, as if this cleared up any and all confusion.

Again, blank faces. Wes yawned.

"I'm a professional footballer," Jack said indignantly. "I play for Manchester United!"

Comprehension dawned on their faces at last. Jack smiled smugly.

"I don't care," said Wes.

Jack stared in surprise.

"Oh no, I don't mean that in a bad way," Wes said. "It's just that, you know, while I'm happy for you and everything, it has absolutely no effect on me whether you're a soccer player or a crossing guard."

"It's football, not soccer," Jack muttered under his breath.

Lesley giggled. "That's amazing that you're a professional, Jack," she said. "That's really, er... So you were saying that you were walking home from a game?"

The footballer composed himself.

"Yeah," he said. "I, er, it was training, actually. I like to walk home because I live pretty close to the centre. Anyway, I was walking through a local park just round from my house. It's quite small, there's a lot of trees and a little pond in the middle, too. I remember sitting on one of the benches, just watching the swans swim about. And... Oh yeah, there was a young boy further up the path, up to the left, and he was wearing a United strip with 'Flint' on the back – that's my name, by the way, my second name – and then... I think, yeah, I think that's the last thing I remember." He stood with his hands on his hips again. "That's weird, isn't it? What did I do after that and why can't I remember?"

A look of horror flashed across his face. "Oh, God, you don't think... If we're dreaming, does that mean I'm lying fast asleep on a bench in the middle of bloody Manchester??"

"Perhaps," answered Teddy, stifling a chuckle.

"What I want to know is – what were you doing sitting on a bench in the park just minutes from your front door? Surely a professional footballer has dozens of bizarre and expensive activities he could be doing instead?"

Jack's face turned a deep shade of crimson. He muttered something inaudible.

"Sorry?" said Teddy, the corners of his mouth twitching. "I didn't catch that."

Jack swallowed and looked up. "I like sitting in the park," he said bluntly, "because people ask me for an autograph, okay? I, er, I dunno, I like the attention." Lesley and Teddy both laughed. Wes smiled and slapped Jack on the shoulder. "At least you're honest, buddy."

Teddy stood up into the sunlight again.

"The last thing I remember," he said. "I was in my office. I was exhausted – it's... it's been a long couple of weeks – so I sat myself down on the sofa. That was what originally convinced me that this is all a dream. But, after hearing your stories, I'm not so sure. However, I really can't think of any other explanation... Other than..." He stopped.

"Other than what?" asked Wes.

"No, it's nothing, I really have no idea," replied Teddy.

He clapped his hands together softly and walked up and down the road. When he turned back to the others, he looked up. There was an uneasy expression on his face – his brow was furrowed, his eyes searched the surroundings, and he chewed his bottom lip nervously.

"I have this really strange feeling that we're being watched," he said. He fidgeted with his hands. "I'm not sure I can put my finger on it, it's just a nagging feeling I have. Like maybe we're not alone."

The nerves spread to the others.

"Well," said Lesley. "It is possible, entirely possible, that we're not alone. Each one of us thought we were by ourselves, and we've all met three new people. I'd say it's likely there are more people around here somewhere. The question is: why are we here? Why were we chosen?"

Jack chewed on a fingernail. "This might sound really stupid," he said. "But we might be part of some reality show? You know, dump some celebrities... and, er, normal people, in the middle of nowhere and watch what happens. They could've set cameras up all over the place."

"It's possible," said Lesley. "But where would they hide the cameras? There's only a few stones and some sand. Also, considering I, and probably these two, didn't sign any contract, then it's tantamount to kidnapping. Unless someone forged our signatures or is setting us up."

"That's what my first thought was," said Wes. "I've got a couple of friends who are crazy enough to do something like that, but I'm not so sure anymore because it's not just me.

"I mean," he continued. "Some of these guys are stone cold psycho but there's no way to grab four people from all over the world. We've got two Americans, an English guy and I'm assuming you're Australian?"

Lesley nodded.

"Come on," said Wes. "Abducting four people from three different countries is beyond just about anyone on the planet, other than governments and, well, yeah, reality show executives. They're the only ones with enough power and crazy enough to actually do it. Personally, now that I've said all that, I'm inclined to believe it's all a dream."

Jack, Lesley, and Teddy nodded.

"There's obviously no evidence that it *is* a dream," Teddy said. "But it seems to be theory that is hardest to fully dismiss."

"This feels too real," said Jack. "I don't like it. But I'll go along with it."

He looked up at the sky where the sun still shone. Peeling out from the road in the far distance were several thicker bushes and trees; there was a distinct green tint just below the horizon.

"So," Jack said, breaking the silence that had lasted longer than he realised. "How do we escape this? How do we wake ourselves up? Any ideas?"

Wes turned and looked over his shoulder in the same direction Jack was facing. Teddy noticed his gaze and sensed the same lingering discontent he, too, experienced.

"I think we should walk along the road," Lesley said. The others turned to face her and she smiled sheepishly.

"I can't explain it; I just have this nagging feeling like... I feel like we should keep going the way we're going." She pointed into the pale distance. "If there are answers, we'll find them down there. I don't know how and I don't know why. It just feels like the right thing to do."

There was unequivocal agreement.

And so they walked along the desolate road, apprehension hovering unpleasantly above them like a thick cloud of dark rain threatening to burst open at any moment. However, the physical action fuelled the determination within them and each step was an act of defiance in the face of the menacing unknown.

Chapter Three

Wes squinted at the sun – it had dipped lower in the sky in the past ten minutes or so but still it pulsed malevolently and beat upon his back. There had been scraps of conversation since they started walking but Wes was oblivious to all of it, lost in broken memories. He thought back to younger days, before the army, when he was a fresh-faced senior and captain of the football team. He had the world at his feet. The future looked abundant, glorious and, above all, certain...

"Where are you from in the States, Wes?" asked Teddy.

Wes was shaken from his reminiscing.

"Huh?" he said. "Were you talking to me?"

"Yeah, I was asking where you're from. I'd guess mid-West?"

"Oh, Kansas."

Wes cleared his throat.

"Yeah, born in Kansas but we moved about a lot. I... my dad, he was an officer, so he wasn't there all the time."

Teddy nodded. "And your mother?"

"Librarian. She loves books. But it didn't pay that well and with my dad away a lot, we ended up on the road for a few years. Amazingly, she managed to get a job at my dad's old high school teaching English, just as I was due to start. It's back in Kansas. We ended up living round the corner from the house I originally grew up in."

"It was rural? Or in the centre?"

"No, it was definitely rural," laughed Wes. "Have you seen Kansas? I lived five minutes from a large farm. My dad knew the farmer. He was football mad and that was absolutely fine with me! We would play games on some of his land with a couple of the farmer's kids. They were good days. Pretty much anytime I said I wanted to play football, dad would manage to round up half the village – there would be about twenty on each side, from kids all the way up to old guys with walking sticks. The mums and the wives would bring food and drink along and set them up on tables. They'd sit on deck chairs, relaxing in the sun. It was like a street party! And my dad, he organised it all. Every time you turned round, he'd be talking to someone new. It was amazing how he brought everyone together, just because his kid wanted to play a game of touch."

Teddy smiled. "Did you tell him?"

Wes looked over at him. "Tell him what?"

"How much it meant it to you. I'm just curious, you understand. I always ask these questions. It's the reason I'm a psychiatrist."

Wes was silent for a moment. He thought back to those days. In the evenings he would sit at the foot of the shabby armchair and watch whatever happened to be on the television. After his dad had helped clear away the mess of the day's events and presented and accepted countless farewells from old and new friends alike, Wes would quickly tidy the living room and await his dad's arrival. They would sit in comfortable silence, occasionally passing remark on the program they were watching or yelling at the screen if it happened to be sports.

His father would often reach his hand over and lay it gently on Wes's head. That was as much affection as they shared, but Wes knew the meaning behind it was more significant than words could say.

"No, not really," he said quietly to Teddy. "I just always assumed he knew. Everyone was always thanking him for stuff, he was so generous."

"I understand. I'm sure he does know. But it means a lot to hear it said, especially when it comes from someone whose very existence you cherish more than your own."

They walked on in silence for another minute. The atmosphere changed abruptly when Jack asked: "You know American football is barely a sport, right?"

Wes guffawed. "What? You kidding me? It's fierce, it's skilful, it's super tough. Try taking hits from 200lb monsters every time you're on the field!"

"Well, that's the thing – you're barely ON the field. There's so many breaks. You start, you stop, you're on, you're off. What's tough about that?"

Wes stopped walking and stared at him. Jack faced him with a glint in his eye. "I'm only kidding," he said. "Well, not really, I do think football - the *real* football - is by far the better sport. But I'll hold my hands up and accept it if you choose yours instead."

"I can understand that Europeans don't really take to it, but it's their loss, believe me. Teddy, you play football, yeah?"

Teddy shook his head. "Thanksgiving, maybe. That's it."

Jack grinned at Wes. "Okay, we'll agree to disagree, cowboy."

He started walking again. Wes studied him as he went. Jack had a hint of a swagger, and a relaxed nature that Wes felt he was incompatible with. How could someone act so nonchalant in such a distressing situation? It was madness. And yet, here was Jack, wandering along the road, without a care for any danger and certainly without a care for any of us, Wes thought.

He started to walk and noticed Lesley looking at him over her shoulder. She had listened intently when he was speaking.

"Do you love football?" she asked. "Do you love playing football?"

Wes nodded. "Yeah, of course. I always have. Although I haven't played for a few years now... not since I left school."

"And how old are you now?"

"Twenty six."

"How come you didn't keep playing?"

Wes smiled ruefully. "It's a long story."

Lesley gestured at the road. "We got a lot of time," she smiled.

There was a long pause. Wes chewed on his lip.

"Okay, alright," he said finally. "I'll tell you my story. I'll keep it short and sweet, though, and just give you the good bits. I don't, er..." He cleared his throat. "I'm not good at opening up about myself, but I'll try my best."

He rubbed his hands together nervously. "So, this is going back to senior year, maybe eight or nine years ago."

There was a nervous anticipation in the air. None of the players would admit it, but the anxiety and tension in the dressing room was palpable.

"I don't need to say much," Coach Quigley was saying. "This is the big one, boys. You've all done fantastic work, you've given me everything to get to the position we're in. And for that, you deserve great credit."

He looked around at the faces. There was stony silence. These boys had steel, grit, and fire in their bones.

"But all that's done now," he continued. "And here we stand today. I'll keep it snappy – win today and that trophy is ours. But that's not all..."

His gaze fell on Wes Dean, the quarterback, the man with the Golden Arm.

"Win today, gentleman, and immortality is yours."

One by one they marched out of the dressing room, grim determination in their eyes. Wes was the last one out. Coach Quigley shook his hand and nodded. The team trooped down the corridor. Near the end, just catching the sunlight from the illuminated exit, there was a glint of gold. Wes approached it and looked longingly inside. The trophy cabinet was an array of bronze, silver, and gold. There were three shelves, each one bursting with medals and pennants. Right in the centre was a large golden trophy, boasting no scratches or stains. The light hit the surface and slid down its smooth shell. Wes smiled at the inscription: "Ryan Dean: Quarterback." He stepped out into a cacophony of noise. Men, women, children — the whole crowd were whipped up into a frenzy, passion oozing from the stands and trickling onto the field where Wes stood stoically, supremely focused. He could feel the hundreds of eyes boring into his back and he knew, without looking, exactly where his father and mother were located. With a long deep breath and a silent prayer, Wes fixed his helmet securely in place. It was game time.

It took about an hour after the match for Wes to finally extricate himself from the relentless throng of blubbering teammates and weeping fans, each one determined to grab a moment with the hero quarterback, before he could seek out his father.

And there he stood, beaming proudly, at the heart of his own little crowd of admirers. The achievements of Ryan Dean were not forgotten in a hurry, not at this school, not in this town.

The next hour was a blur, full of smiles and delirium, and, eventually, before he knew it, Wes was sitting in his favourite spot in the small living room back home. He quietly reflected on the game and celebrations. With the tie hanging in the balance in the dying seconds, Wes collected the ball and slung his arm forward like the crack of a whip. His unblinking eyes followed the trajectory and he watched, in a state akin to disbelief, as the ball landed comfortably in his teammate's hands deep into the end zone.

A moment of infinite silence. Time seemed suspended as if it, too, was comprehending the climax to the match.

And then came the explosion of noise. A sea of red and gold flowed down from the surrounding stands, swarming towards one man, eager to praise the new hero.

Wes smiled at the memory. After the hundreds of fans were all satisfied, Wes slipped through the crowd now singing his name and made his way outside the stadium. There stood his father boasting a warm smile that stretched from ear to ear. Wes embraced his father and held him tight; he understood his dad was communicating his pride. No words were needed.

Ryan released Wes and wiped a shallow tear from his eye. He looked at his son and thought about his future. Wes could go on to college and play. He could coach - the boy was a born leader. Should he choose to accept the military life, he would excel, no question about it. But it was a lonely life, considered Ryan. He had neglected Wes because of his own commitments. And he did not want his son to do the same.

He smiled and opened his mouth to speak. Wes, you can lead and inspire, he thought. You can change the world.

But, then again, the kid probably knew it already.

"Son," he said. "It looks like they're gonna give you a trophy to keep mine company."

Wes chuckled. His father placed his hand on his head and led him towards the car.

There was a 'bang!' from the television which jerked Wes backed to his senses. It was an old documentary about one of the wars. He was still sitting at the foot of his dad's chair, waiting for his father to come in and give his own commentary on the match.

He heard frantic whispers coming from the kitchen. His mother and father were having a heated debate about something.

"...Ryan, you have to tell him. Now."

"The boy's just won the championship, he's on a high, I can't do that to--"

"What? And wait for tomorrow? There's no time! Get in there now."

"But, I--"

"Ryan. Now."

There was a moment of silence and then the sound of shuffling feet. Wes turned his head away from the kitchen and focused intently on the television.

Seconds later, his dad appeared. He hesitated when he reached Wes, as if he had never set foot in the room before.

"Er, Wes, son," he said. "Why don't you take a seat over there, I've got some, some news for you."

Wes rose uneasily. He felt his insides squirm. This could not be good, he thought, as he sank into the old sofa.

"So," his dad said. "You know I've been home for a while now. From the Middle East."

Wes nodded silently. He could feel what was coming.

"Well, yeah, I know I've not been home that long, a few months I think."

Wes nodded again. Two months and eight days, in fact.

His father paused. His eyes darted around the room, as if looking for the words.

"I received my summons this morning, son."

He looked at Wes and placed a hand on his knee.

"I have to report for duty tomorrow at dusk."

Wes felt a swooping sensation in his stomach. His insides has stopped churning and now felt completely empty and numb. He could not look his father in his eyes. All he could do was nod.

They stood up at the same time.

"I... It's not fair," mumbled Wes.

"I know, son, I know."

"I thought you were too old to be recalled."

Ryan let out a chuckle. "Ooh, thanks, dude. Thanks a lot"

Wes smiled weakly. "Sorry, no, I just thought you wouldn't be going back..."

"I joined late, remember? I was in my late twenties so I had to stay one more year to retire and get my pension. Obviously I was hoping for a quiet year, but... well, it is what it is. Duty calls."

Wes muttered something about going to bed; he turned to leave the room.

Ryan clasped his arm and pulled him in. He placed his hand squarely on Wes's head and held him tight. He could feel his son shaking slightly and knew there were tears in his eyes. Wes's face was buried deep in Ryan's shoulder.

"I'm sorry, Wes," Ryan sniffed. "I'm sorry."

They held each other close for some time. There was a melancholic understanding between them. Ryan had felt it earlier that day when he first opened the letter of summons. And now Wes was slowly beginning to realise, too. Despite trying to dispel the wretched thought from his mind, he could not escape the morose conclusion. His father would not be coming back.

*

Teddy patted Wes on the back. Wes appreciated the gesture. He nodded silently.

Lesley sniffed. "I'm sorry, Wes."

"What happened, if you don't mind me asking?" said
Teddy

"No, I don't mind. I'm really proud of what he did,
his service to his country, and to his community. I
just..." he stuttered. "I just wish he was still around
when... people... need him now more than ever."
He looked into the deep blue sky. The colour had
waned ever so slightly.

"He left for Afghanistan the next day," Wes
continued. "He and a couple of others got separated
on a patrol and were ambushed. Only two made it
back out of about ten or eleven. My dad-- he actually
made it out of the fighting but couldn't make it all the
way back. And he refused to be a burden to the guys.
The two guys, the survivors, said my dad had kept
everyone positive, which I don't doubt, and one of
the men said my dad saved his life. He pulled him
out of the way of artillery fire or something."
He smiled sadly and kicked some dust up from the
road.

"It was his last tour. He was due back about a week
later."

Lesley wiped tears from her eyes.

"He sounds like a great man," said Teddy.

"You betcha," Wes muttered. "The village really felt it. Everyone was in mourning for ages. But it wasn't until things settled down that you really saw the difference."

"What do you mean?"

"Well, life went on. People went back to their routines and it was like my dad was forgotten. I really missed those games he used to organise, though. Not just because I loved football, but because it brought everyone in the community together. He had this amazing, attractive personality, my dad, and it brought strangers together and turned them into friends. Without him... Well, they just went back to being strangers again."

He looked off into the distance. He thought about the time the first time he met the farmer who lived round the corner. Wes had been playing in the field in front of the farm house. There was the sound of a door crashing open and the farmer came storming out. He was livid.

Wes, frozen with fear, watched helplessly as the farmer bounded towards him, hurling angry words and threats in his direction. Then Wes heard his father's voice. It was as if he had appeared from thin air. He walked with his hands in his pockets, looking, for all the world, like he was off for an afternoon stroll to pick flowers.

"Walter!" he called out cheerfully. "How are you? How are those rascals of yours?"

The next five minutes were a blur. Before he knew it, Wes had a glass of lemonade thrust into his hand by the laughing farmer. Then there was a table set up with hamburgers.

Two boys about Wes's age appeared next to him with a football of their own.

"You're a bit small to play football, aren't you?" the older one said.

Wes looked at his dad. His dad winked and said, "Show 'em what you got."

"And you gave up football after that?" asked Jack.

"Yep," said Wes, abruptly recalled to the present.

"Why?" Jack asked.

Teddy looked squarely at Jack. "Weren't you listening to the story?"

"Yes, of course, but I just don't fully understand." He turned to Wes. "You were clearly good at it and it sounds like you could've gone to college on a scholarship or something."

"Jack," hissed Lesley.

"What? I'm sorry, Wes, about your dad. I really am. But I don't get why you chucked it after that."

Wes stared at him blankly. "Seriously?"

"What?"

"Just because you're good at something," Wesley said. "It doesn't mean you should do it."

"Yeah, that's fair enough," said Jack. "But you keep saying you love football, so--"

"I said I *loved* football. And I did. I lived and breathed football. But I came full circle that day. My dad was my hero. And I matched him. My trophy sits next to his. But I never wanted to beat him."

Jack was puzzled.

"If my dad hadn't died, then yeah, I might've continued playing. I would've gone to college – the offers were there – and I could've put him in my shadow. But why would I want to do a thing like that?

"I realised there's more to life, more to *my* life, than football. My passion for it was tied up in wanting to achieve what my dad achieved. But without him, I realised I had taken football as far as I could... Or rather, football had taken *me* as far as *it* could."

"So what did you do?" asked Jack.

"I went looking for my passion. I went looking for the thing that would fulfil me. The thing that would make me fully understand myself in a way football didn't let me."

Teddy smiled. "So you joined the army?"

Wes nodded.

"Is the army your passion?"

Wes hesitated. "Sure. I mean, I think so."

"Why did you join? How did you know this was right for you?"

"It's the best way for me to honour my father's memory. I get to serve him as well as my country."

"That certainly is honourable. But then surely you're living out *his* passion and not your own?"

Wes opened his mouth to argue but Teddy continued.

"If you're dad was as good a man as you say he was, then I am sure he would not want you to simply follow in his footsteps. He would want you to walk your own path. It is the great hope all parents have."

"Well, you didn't know him," snapped Wes. "And you don't know me!"

"Yes," said Teddy. "You're right. I don't know you. And I don't know your life. But, in my opinion, the best way to honour your father is not by replicating his journey to the letter. It is by embarking on your own journey. This is how you serve your father. This is how you change your world."

Wes sighed and exhaled slowly.

"I'm sorry," he muttered after a long pause. "I didn't mean to... I just, I'm not sure where to start."

"I can think of one place you could begin," said Jack.

Wes turned to look at him. "Where?"

"Those games in your community your dad used to spontaneously organise. Do those still take place?"
Wes shook his head. "Not for a few years now."
"Well, why don't you organise one? It wouldn't be difficult. The people would still remember them – they haven't changed."
"But my dad--"
"--would be proud of you," finished Lesley.
The others nodded. Wes cleared his throat and looked towards the green horizon.

Chapter Four

"Is it just me or is it a little cooler than it was earlier?" The blank sky was still a deep blue but slightly paler than it had been. A light breeze slowly dribbled across the sand, steadily lifting flecks of dust above the feet of the travellers. The road had not wavered – it trudged perennially forwards without a hint of a curve to either side.

"Speak for yourself," replied Jack. I'm burning up."

"That's because you've got a mop-top on your head, holding all the heat in," said Wes. "Come on, man. Get a haircut."

"Ha-bloody-ha. Will I just pop along to the hairdressers hiding behind one of these rocks?" Lesley glanced behind. "I have that horrible feeling again. Like we're being watched. I can't put my finger on it. It feels really strange. To tell you the truth, I'm... I'm getting pretty worried."

"I know," Teddy nodded. "Although I wouldn't be too worried, Lesley, because there doesn't seem anything we can do about it."

"What does that mean?" asked Lesley, perplexed.

"Well," said Teddy. "We're not sure where we are. And we're not sure where to go - where we're *supposed* to go, if you like. And all we have to rely on is gut instinct, right?"

"Yes," said Lesley slowly.

Teddy laughed. "Well, how's that different from life?"

"It's not the same," said Jack.

"Why not? Why isn't it the same? If you take a step back and look at this non-subjectively, what's the difference? Hell, as far as I'm concerned, we're pioneers!"

"You can't do that. We have lives of our own, a world we have known our whole lives. You can't just go about thinking of all this in that way."

"Why not?" said Teddy again. "Look, I understand this is a bizarre place – it's new, it's scary. But we can't shrink away from the challenge that faces us now."

"What challenge?"

"Why, the challenge to survive! The challenge to escape – to get home! I don't know exactly how or when we'll get back but I'm not going to give up. I'm not going to let anxiety cloud my senses or make me give in."

"But aren't you afraid?"

"Of course I am, Jack – I'm terrified! But why should that stop me? Fear is the jailer that keeps hope imprisoned. Bravery sets hope free. And now it's time for us to be brave."

Wes laughed. "You're cracked, you are."

"Probably," Teddy agreed with a smile. "But this is an adventure! I don't want to be a coward any longer. Even if I die and don't make it out--"

"Whoa!" interjected Jack. "Don't say that."

"Say what?"

"That! Don't say we're going to die. That's horrible."

"I'm just saying, it's possible that--"

"Well, don't. You don't know. You don't know that's going to happen. I was fine thinking this is all a dream, but you just make it worse when you come out with stuff like that."

"Look, I'm sorry," Teddy said, apologising to each of them. "I was thinking earlier, and I thought that there's a possibility, a slim, slim chance that this place could be... It could be, maybe, a version of purgatory."

Lesley gasped and recoiled in horror. Wes's eyes widened. Jack clamped his hands over his ears and shouted "No! Shut up!"

"Come off it, Jack," said Teddy, pulling Jack's arms down. "Don't be so childish."

"I'm not being childish," he hissed in reply. "I just don't want you saying we're all dead or dying or whatever. It's morbid. It's grotesque."

Teddy heaved a sigh. "Okay, I'm sorry. Truly, I am. I didn't mean to scare you but it's been playing on my mind since I woke up here."

The others did not meet his gaze.

"Look, we need to discuss this. We don't have to go into too much detail but we need to at least accept it as one of a number of theoretical scenarios."

He paused for a moment and let the idea sink into their minds. They had to be aware.

"Can we talk about this, just for two minutes, please?"

Lesley was the first to raise her head. She looked at the other two who were staring resolutely at the ground.

"He's right," she said. "We have to discuss it. I don't like it. The idea scares me, but... Come on."

Jack and Wes looked at each other then all gazes fixed on Teddy.

"This better be good, Doc" Wes said, his voice slightly higher than normal.

Teddy smiled weakly. "Thank you. Believe me – I'm just as concerned as the rest of you. I've just thought about it for longer so I've had more time to process it."

He rubbed his chin thoughtfully, contemplating where to begin.

"Alright," he said finally. "I think it's pretty clear we've been brought here for a reason. There's obviously still a chance that we're here by accident – I don't know, maybe a teleporter or cryogenic super-sleep or ultra-sleepwalking with some block amnesia thrown in or something equally absurd – but I think that's unlikely, especially since we spawned within walking distance of each other at around about the same time. This leads me to believe that we've been collected or kidnapped. Either way, we've been brought here for something. I don't think there's anything particularly special about us so I seriously doubt we're here to save the world in some doomsday scenario."

Jack sighed. "I'm barely following what you're saying, man. You're just making sounds now, they're barely even words."

Lesley shushed him.

"Anyway," Teddy continued. "Maybe it's not reality – I personally believe it's a dream of some kind – but there's a chance it's something else. Perhaps this is the place lost souls come when... when they're finished their journey on Earth. Before Heaven or Hell. Maybe this is the judgement phase. And we will be judged on what we do in this strange new land."

His words slid off into silence. The only sound was the whispering wind and the nervous shuffle of Jack's feet. At long last, Lesley spoke:

"I don't want it to be true."

Her voice was weak and timid but it grew stronger as she talked.

"I appreciate and accept the possibility, Teddy. But I don't agree with it. Mainly because I think it is more likely to be a dream or some artificial reality. But I also disagree with it because I simply don't like it. It frightens me. I don't want it to be true."

Wes stepped forward. "You're right Lesley. I don't think it's true. To be honest, it doesn't feel right. Sure, this place is totally alien so nothing feels right but..." he considered for a moment. "No, it doesn't feel like purgatory. This isn't my time to die."

"What do you mean: 'It's not my time to die'?" Jack asked, bewildered.

Wes looked at him and shrugged. "My story isn't over yet, Jack."

And with that he turned and resumed walking. The others trudged along in his wake, only slightly comforted by the soldier's puzzling words.

Lesley began walking again, no more at ease than she originally was. Inside she was a jumble of emotions and thoughts, twisting and intertwining until she could not make head or tail of either. She glanced behind again. There were a few more trees but they were too thin for anyone to hide behind. The rocks were large enough for someone to comfortably remain unseen but they were now few and far between and there was no way for someone to dart between each one. Lesley looked all around to confirm there was nothing – and no-one – out of the ordinary. Yet still she felt a familiar paranoia that made the hairs on the back of her neck stand up. She bowed her head shamefully. All her life she had been dogged by self-doubt and even here, even now, she felt vulnerable due to her own lack of conviction. Was it possible that they were in a purgatory of some sort? Her life had barely begun. She was only in her twenties. There should have been loads of time for her to do the things she really wanted. All those dreams and aspirations: at one point they seemed like high rungs on a ladder; now they were shimmers – wisps of clouds, dissipating into everything and nothing all at once.

Fear fed off her like a hungry parasite. It stalked her as a shadow. It was the voice in her ear, countering ambition at every turn. It stole her voice in the moments it mattered. Lesley grew up alone and lonely, drifting in and out of a life of silence and solitude.

But she was brilliant. Undeniably. Her teachers knew it. The orphanage where she was raised recognised her gifts early on and provided what meagre resources they could to aid her development. Not only was she a girl of particular talent academically with a memory that astounded her peers and professionals alike, but she also had an exceptionally kind and generous disposition. Her heart was so soft it floated like a feather and despite her lack of participation in any consistent social circle, she was never victimised or bullied. Other children were aware of her outsider status but it was not a cause, or reason, for violence. They felt her lonely charm and were richer for being in her presence.

Lesley smiled at the memory of her formative years. She did not have an unhappy childhood. It was what came afterwards that plunged her into uncertainty.

"Lesley?"

She looked up at the sound of her name. Teddy was looking back at her with his brow furrowed.

"Are you okay?" he asked.

"Huh? Yeah. Why?"

"I was just asking if you still lived in Australia. You said you were originally from there but your accent seems a little affected."

"Oh, sorry, I was miles away," she said.

"I wish I was," muttered Jack under his breath.

"I was born in Australia but I live in the UK now."

"Ah, okay, and what do you do now?"

"I work for a bank. I, well, the company, dabble in the stock exchange, predict trends and so on. Er..." she trailed off.

"So you're a big bucks hotshot?" joked Wes.

"Hardly," replied Lesley blushing. "I'm just a secretary. Although I do know a little bit about banking."

"From things you've picked up on the job?"

"No, I studied it at university," she mumbled.

"Oh, really?" said Teddy. "I hope you don't mind me prying, but was the degree not good enough to become a fully fledged banking associate?"

Lesley coughed. "Um, well, actually... I... it was mathematics, statistics, finance and economics. I got my masters from... Oxford."

Teddy let out a low whistle. "Wow, impressive."

"So why didn't you get the big job? Or at least go for something a little more... impressive given your degree?" asked Wes.

Lesley shrugged, blushing harder than ever. "I dunno, it just..."

"I mean, there's nothing wrong with being a secretary, of course," Wes said hurriedly. "That's, that's great if it's what you want to do. I just thought people like you – clever people, I mean – would be cleaning up in job interviews, running the country, blowing money on the stock markets or whatever."

"Is that what you wanted to be when you were younger?" asked Jack.

Lesley thought for a minute. "No," she said. "It's just something that happened. I always..."

She trailed off.

"Go on," urged Wes kindly.

She swallowed. "Well, I always wanted to volunteer and help other people who weren't as fortunate. I don't mean travel, although that would be a definite benefit, I'll admit, but going to people who are in desperate need of help and offering them what I can. That doesn't just mean going off to the four corners of the Earth looking for a thrilling adventure. It's not about that. I genuinely just want to help make the world a little bit better. I... I know it sounds like I'm running for Miss World when I say it like that--" she giggled through her embarrassment "--but I always wanted to give something back, to repay a debt I owe."

The others listened intently. Lesley appreciated their silence and took advantage of it before continuing. "I remember my mother's smile the last time I saw her. My father stared at her like a lost man stares at the stars – he was so swept away in awe and wonder. The two stood side by side, looking like clouds in a dream. They walked out of the door, promising they wouldn't be late home. I fell asleep that night with the image of them the last thing on my mind. When I woke up, I knew immediately from the babysitter's wails what had happened. I didn't need to see the police..."

Snow drifted listlessly across the dawn sky. The small park was draped in a soft blanket of white. In the early morning daylight the snow lay, untouched and untrampled, on the ground. The smooth, rolling mounds of grass were asleep amidst the gentle flurry of delicate flakes. The only noise came from the tender swaying of branches in the ever-so-slight breeze.
Lesley stood alone at the entrance to the park, watching the fairytale scene unfold. She was the only person in the whole world.

She ventured forward, feeling the light crunch beneath her feet as she landed on the squashed snow. Her breath released in a mist of white and floated towards the heavens. With every step she disappeared further into the landscape, following the winding road that was free of fresh footprints. When she reached the old fountain in the centre of the park she turned to face it slowly.

Her parents had taken her here every year when the first snows fell.

Lesley looked up at the statue perched at the height of the fountain. In the summer, it was no more than a repugnant gargoyle, an eroded fiend, desecrated by time. At the start of winter, however, Lesley's father would take her hand and point to the monument as it was coated in a pure glaze of white, pervading every crevice on the surface and accentuating a soft allure the statue seemed to have relinquished many years before. The timid sunlight struck it and the transformation was complete: the highlights and shadows merged seamlessly and Lesley saw the graceful beauty of the lonely angel. It smiled sadly.

"Everything has beauty, Lesley," her father had whispered.

A despondent tear trickled down Lesley's face as she faced the angel, two lonely souls sharing a secluded peace.

Lesley turned as she heard the sound of hurried footsteps, crunching through the snow. Rushing towards her was the frantic figure of Miss Eleanor, Maria, from the orphanage. "Lesley!" she cried out in relief. "I've been so worried about you!"

She stopped just short of Lesley when she saw her heavy red eyes. Maria knelt down and smiled. She held her arms out and beckoned her in. They held each other close for what seemed like an eternity. Maria considered their surroundings.

"This is a beautiful place, Lesley. How did you find it?"

The girl looked down and swallowed slowly. Maria knew what she was going to say but let her speak.

"M-my mum and dad used to take me here to see the snow."

"I can see why. You should have mentioned it so you could take me here as well. I didn't know it was so... It's like a fairytale, isn't it? Peaceful, untouched... And that is the most elegant angel I have ever seen."

Lesley smiled and remained still as Maria produced a tissue and wiped her tears away.

"Do we have to go back now?" asked Lesley quietly. She listened carefully for the response. Still only the branches swayed, everywhere else was silence.

"Everyone has been worried about you, Lesley. Do you know they've split up into search and rescue parties for you?"

Lesley shook her head. "I'm sorry, I didn't mean for you to organise..."

"Us? No, not the adults – we didn't get a chance to! It was the other children who suggested it. They care about you a lot. We're a family, you know. Every single one of us."

She paused and looked at Lesley's wide, brown eyes. The little girl was scared, lost, and lonely. There was a torment inside her, a scar that would take a long time to heal. But heal it would.

"Why don't we stay a little longer? We have all the time in the world. You can tell me all about the park, and share some stories from here from when you were a little younger."

She held out her hand.

"Or we can simply walk in silence."

Lesley hesitated and then a fresh tear ran down her face. "I just miss them so much," she wept helplessly.

"I know, I know," said Maria, holding her close as she sobbed into her shoulder. "It's a horrible pain and it's a burden you should never have had to bare."

She wiped the tears away from Lesley's face again and smiled warmly. "You know... The ones we love never truly leave us," she said. "Look around, Lesley. Look where you are. Why did you come here? Because of your parents. Why did you stop at this fountain? Because they brought you here before. And I bet you look at that downtrodden angel and you feel overcome by its lonely beauty.

"You have such compassion inside you, Lesley. Your generous heart can soften stone. But it wasn't something you were born with."

Lesley looked at her and then at the statue atop the fountain.

"Your mother and father live on within you."

Lesley took her hand and they slowly walked through the snow.

*

"...and of course, the beautiful quote that describes the two lovers: 'Eternity was in our lips and eyes.' So, what can we deduce from these descriptions?"

Mrs Eliza looked up from her copy of *Antony & Cleopatra* and watched the engaged faces of her English class contort themselves in thought as the students pondered an answer.

Lesley attempted an answer. English was the only class she spoke in.

"That Antony and Cleopatra are in love?"

"That's the understatement of the century, Harper."

There was a ripple of laughter throughout the class. Lesley joined in.

"What we can deduce, cherubs, is that Antony and Cleopatra are a couple of drama queens!"

More laughter. The bell sounded, echoing through the corridors. The class groaned.

"Okay," Mrs Eliza said. "That's your lot, folks. Off you pop. For homework, go and act out some scenes of the play in your room. And do all the different voices too."

The class filed out reluctantly. Lesley was one of the last ones to leave but she turned when the teacher called out her name.

"Lesley," began Mrs Eliza when all the students had left the room. "Have you been thinking about university? I know it's way, way, way in the distant future of the next six months and you've got exams before then... but have you made any decisions yet?"

Lesley shook her head. Mrs Eliza was very helpful at giving advice but she always stopped short of telling Lesley exactly what to do. Sometimes Lesley resented this and she really wished her favourite teacher would just decide for her. The indecision preyed on her constantly.

"Have you considered English?"

Lesley nodded. "Of course I have," she smiled.

"Good, I think you'd be terrific at it. You have talent, clearly, and an original voice in your prose. Don't tell anyone but you're top the class by a country mile, and this isn't a class of numbskulls. Well, okay, there are several numbskulls..."

Lesley giggled.

"Think about it. You'd be excellent at any subject but don't rush into anything. Who knows? University might not be right for you. Remember, there's a life beyond academia. Don't get me wrong – it is absolutely paramount to a person's, particularly a child's, development, but there are lessons to learn that can't be found in books."

Lesley stared, hanging on her every word. She thought about what her teacher was saying but she still wasn't sure... If I don't go to university, what should I do?

"Do what makes you happy," Mrs Eliza said, as if reading Lesley's mind. "Find your passion and immerse yourself in it. Your heart knows the way so always trust your instincts. And remember: there is a beauty in doing what you love. There is nothing more inspiring than a person with passion."

Lesley walked to her next class with Mrs Eliza's words echoing in her head.

Mathematics was a blur for the next hour. Lesley eased through the subject. She enjoyed maths.

Before she knew it, she was leaving the classroom. It was like déjà vu as the teacher called out her name. Lesley turned and approached Mr Foster. He was undoing his burgundy bow-tie. Mr Foster was very well liked by his students, too. His energy and excitement was contagious but his pupils really fed off his genuineness; he did not claim to be infallible and often laughed at his own mistakes.

"Damn thing nearly chokes me," he said, laying the bow-tie down on his desk.

He turned his attention to Lesley. "So, how are you, chicken?"

Lesley smiled. "I'm fine, sir, thanks."

"Are you sure? Any problems at all?"

She shook her head.

"Good," Mr Foster smiled. "Well, Lesley, how is the university application going?"

She didn't answer but pulled a pained expression.
"Ah," he said. "That bad, huh?"
He picked up a stack of old textbooks from his desk and carried them to the cupboard at the back of the classroom. Lesley looked around. It was probably the messiest classroom in the school and very little of that was down to the students. There were posters all over the walls, overlapping each other, competing for visibility. Textbooks, worksheets, rulers and calculators were left abandoned on different tables. And Mr Foster's desk was home to a mountain of paperwork. When he sat behind it, which rarely happened, he would disappear entirely from view.
"How do you feel," he called from the cupboard, head buried in one of the shelves, "about maths?"
Lesley watched as he extricated himself from the textbooks and eventually perched himself dangerously on the edge of his own desk at the front. The pile of papers teetered.
"I like it," replied Lesley truthfully. "It's one of my favourite subjects."
"Ah, come on, now, you're just trying to make me blush!" Mr Foster laughed, and then grew serious. "What do you think about studying it at university?"

Lesley was taken aback. She had never thought about it. In all honesty, she did not even think about university that much. Not in detail anyway. It was just a looming, threatening shadow in her mind she never addressed but allowed to fester and fill her with steady dread.

"The thing is, Lesley, it's a really safe subject to study. There's *always* jobs going for maths graduates, and for someone with brains like yours? You'd clean up!"

She stared at him blankly.

"If you study maths, you could easily pick up some finance and accounting on the side. If you do well enough, you could do a masters year at Cambridge." He studied Lesley closely. "I wouldn't advise this if you weren't keen on maths, you understand. It's important to enjoy what you do. That's the main reason I think this could be the right path for you. A maths degree opens up so many doors."

Lesley thought about it. It did seem to be logical. She would be set for a career path. It was only four or five years, she would still be young when she finished. And, most tempting of all, it would release the knot in her stomach the uncertainty of her future had placed there.

"What do you think?" Mr Foster asked with a smile.

Lesley gulped. "I do like maths..." she mumbled.

Mr Foster nodded. "I'll tell you what – I'll write your reference for you. And I have a few friends at different universities around the country. You'll be taken care of, Lesley. What do you say?"

Lesley thought about it. At least she wouldn't have to worry all the time. The uncertainty scared her terribly. But she could be rid of it now. Right now. No more worrying...

She nodded. "Yeah, yes, that's... thank you, Mr Foster."

He smiled warmly and patted her arm. "I'm excited for you. I really am. Just work hard, and keep being you."

Lesley turned to leave and she had reached the door when Mr Foster called her name again.

"Yes, sir?"

He paused for a moment. He noticed Lesley's lonely eyes. She was a special person and a special student. The kind of pupil that took lessons to heart. One who makes the job worthwhile. Mr Foster, like Mrs Eliza and many others, would miss her when she was gone.

"If you ever need anything, anything at all, Lesley, you know where I am," he said. "You're not alone. We're all in this together."

Lesley smiled.

"Right now, chop chop, off to class, Harper, you lazy layabout."

He winked and sank into his desk chair. Lesley giggled and, as she walked down the corridor, she was sure she heard a pile of papers collapse and spill over the floor.

Chapter Five

The road had widened slightly as they continued walking. On both sides of the trail, trees and bushes became more abundant; these were not the decrepit logs and rotten wood they had passed earlier but trees of sturdy, rich brown trunks more than six or seven feet tall. Each branch had a number of dark orange and green leaves, happily swaying in the breeze. Patches of grass had sprung up too. They grew sparsely yet resolutely amongst the sand and were several feet across. None of the patches had encroached upon the road, however. It was still as blank and empty as always, a smooth paint stroke along the canvas of the wasteland.

Teddy smiled consolingly at Lesley as she wiped her eyes clean.

"I've never told anyone that before," she said at last. Teddy pondered for a moment. "Sometimes it's easier to open up to strangers. You don't have a personality or persona to reinforce and you speak without fear of judgement."

He stopped talking when Wes gave him a look full of significance.

"Er," Teddy hesitated. "Maybe you just feel a connection with us."

Lesley nodded silently and they could sense she was comforted.

Jack coughed. "I would offer to make you a cup of tea but, er, I left my kettle in the other desert next door."

Lesley laughed and cleared her throat. She looked around again out of habit and spoke uneasily. "I don't like these trees. Well, they're better than the sand and desert, but they're too... big. Anyone, or anything could hide behind it."

Wes glanced around nervously. Neither he nor Teddy spoke. Jack, however, dashed off to the nearest tree and attempted to hide his lean frame behind the trunk of a gnarly looking specimen.

"Come on," he shouted, his voice muffled and echoing slightly. "There's no way someone could hide behind here. Look," he waved his arms. "You can see me now, right? And I'm barely moving!"

He poked his head out and wore a silly grin.

"If I was following us, I'd have to poke my head out every two minutes to check where we were, then sprint to another tree or rock."

He spilled out from behind the tree into a forward roll.

"You'd have to be a bloody ninja to carry that off."

The tension was burst as the others laughed. Jack brushed the sand out of his hair and filed back in on the road.

"Do you mind if I ask you a question, Lesley?" asked Wes.

"No, of-of course not," she said with a hint of anxiety.

"Why did you go to an orphanage? Did you not have other family members?"

"No," she replied quietly. "They, um, there was an aunt I'd never met who lived in the UK but I was in Australia at the time."

"Ah, okay. And they didn't want to send you halfway across the globe?"

"I..." she stuttered. "I... Obviously they didn't want to uproot me, even though I'd been to the country before. But they asked me what I wanted. I was nine at the time and I didn't want to leave my parents' country, or city."

She waited for another question but Wes stayed quiet. He stared straight ahead – he was uncomfortable asking too much about other people's lives. Lesley continued.

"I had – have – a lot of memories from there. It's my home. And I didn't want to forget the person I was with my parents."

Teddy spoke. "You said you wanted to give something back. Do you mean give something back to the orphanage in that community?"

"Yes, I owe them everything. But I think I was lucky, well, in a morbid, roundabout sort of way. I suffered a tragedy and these amazing people took me in. They saved my life. And yet, there's thousands of children, not just orphans, who are lost and alone and even dying. I feel compelled to help them. One way or another, I owe something to the world. And these children deserve a chance at life."

Her head was bowed and her face flushed as she spoke from her heart.

"I remember Maria, the woman from the orphanage, saying that, although she felt genuine pride and fulfilment in her job, it was never enough for her to consider her work complete. I remember asking her if she ever thought about retiring and she said 'There's always more people to rescue, more lives to save. And the kindness these children encounter here will stay with them forever. When they grow up, their generosity and compassion will move mountains.'

"I believe that, one child at a time, she saves the world."

Her words streamed off into silence. Eventually, Wes spoke.

"That's beautiful, Lesley."

Jack laid a hand on her shoulder and squeezed firmly. She looked up with fresh tears in her eyes and returned Jack's warm smile.

"Those are very inspiring words," said Teddy. "And I really do agree with them. I just wondered, though..."

He avoided Wes's gaze and looked down at the ground for several seconds.

"What?" asked Lesley.

"Well, I just wondered... You obviously believe in this cause, and you have first-hand experience of knowing what these children go through."

"Yes, of course."

He paused for a second and then looked up and locked gazes with her.

"So... what are you doing working in a bank?" he asked.

The silence had returned. They held a steady pace as the greenery thickened around them. Jack shuffled his feet to make a little noise but it eventually echoed into nothing. The absence of sound seemed to amplify. The eerie stillness heightened the apprehension in the air. The eyes of everyone darted all around looking for some sign of familiarity to quell their unease.

"I don't like this," said Jack.

Wes nodded in agreement. "This feels really strange all of a sudden. I know everything about this is strange and weird, but... I don't know," he grunted in frustration. "The air feels so close with these trees as well, and... I have that horrible, horrible feeling, like there's a crosshair square on my back."

Lesley fidgeted fretfully.

"It's probably nothing," said Teddy aloofly. "You might have claustrophobia, Wes. It can be exac--"

"I don't have goddamn claustrophobia, doc, okay??" Wes snapped.

He stopped walking and turned to face Teddy. "And I wish you'd stop going on, pontificating about your theories and your ideas. You don't know what's going on so maybe it'd be better if you stopped trying to freak everyone out just so you can sound so smart all the time!"

"I'm just saying that--"

"Well DON'T '*just say*'! It does no-one any good. You're mad you are."

He spat on the ground.

Teddy turned to Lesley. "Lesley, you know I'm speaking sense. There's no point--"

"Yes," said Lesley, not looking at him. "But, Wes is right. You don't have to vocalise every thought, especially if you're just trying to scare us. And you don't need to pass judgement on everything and... and everyone."

He looked at her in shock. "What? You're taking his side?"

He could feel the frustration and anger rising inside him and it was drowning out his common sense. Of course he could have been a little more tactful with what he said, but if they were going to act so immature about it and whimper at the first sign of distress... He was the qualified professional after all. "I can't believe this," he said venomously.

"Look," said Jack. "I don't want to cause a confrontation and think we should stick together here. I think Teddy is right--" Wes opened his mouth to angrily reply, but Jack hurried on. "--I think he's right in some of the things he's said. But," he turned to Teddy. "You need to ease up a bit, man."

Jack smiled and let out a nervous chuckle. "You know? You're just getting a bit excited, I dunno. Maybe you should just dial it back a little bit?"

Teddy stared at him in an embittered rage. The emotions of the last few hours were building in everyone and the irritation was bubbling to the surface.

"I'm sorry," he spat. "But what do you actually bring to the table here, Jack? You just kick a ball. You've not helped in the slightest, you don't have ideas, you don't share. What is the point of you??"

Jack was stunned into a momentary silence.

"That's enough," said Wes.

And then everyone was arguing at once. Wes and Jack were cutting across each other to yell at Teddy. Teddy was confronting Lesley, his arms windmilling about in fury. The noise echoed off the ground and the rocks until it felt like there were more people shouting.

As the four of them vented their exasperation and anger, none of them heard the soft footsteps approaching from behind them.

The wind swept more swiftly across the ground, blowing leaves off of the trees and sand onto the road. The leaves were a blur of autumnal orange as they billowed around the heads of the arguing group. Eventually the wind was loud enough to drown out their shouts. The echoes lingered and died as the wind decreased.

It was then that they heard the soft, female voice. It felt mystical and ethereal, barely more than a whisper and yet reverberating potently across the hollow plain.

"Hello travellers," it spoke. "Are you lost?"

Chapter Six

Along the dusty road walked a graceful figure. She approached the group with soft steps. Elegance was in her movements, she almost seemed to glide. Her flowing black hair shone brightly in the sun and the deep pools of blue in her eyes matched the sky. A subdued smile played upon her lips as she studied the four arguing strangers.

They were struck dumb after hearing her speak and stared in suspicious silence until Wes regained his composure.

"Hello," he said, clearing his throat. "What, um... Are you okay? Are you, um, are *you* lost?"

He glanced at the others and hesitated before continuing.

"Because we can help... we think," he smiled nervously.

There was something different about this woman, however. She didn't appear to be like the others who had woken up, confused and alarmed, in a strange place. She didn't even look lost.

"Yes, that's right," Teddy spoke with authority. "You can come with... us."

He paused as if the woman had shushed him herself. Finally she spoke.

"You don't appear to know what you're doing," she said plainly, her eyes slowly passing from person to person.

Wes and Teddy started and prepared to argue their position but Lesley cut across them.

"She's right," she said. "There's no point lying and pretending we actually know what's going on."

Lesley turned to the woman.

"The truth is: we all woke up with no recollection of how and when we got here. We all met just a couple of hours ago and we've been going along this road ever since. I don't... We can't tell anything more than that, it's all just guesswork. We don't have an explanation, none of us know where we are and there's--"

"I know where we are," the woman calmly interrupted.

There was a collective gasp.

"What?" spluttered Teddy. "Where? How do you know?"

"Did... did you bring us here?" asked Lesley, her kidnapping theory coming to the forefront of her mind again.

"You brought yourselves here," the woman answered cryptically.

"And what's that supposed to mean?" grunted Wes.
The woman didn't answer. She stared coolly at Wes.
"God, I really hate riddles," he said impatiently.
Jack had remained silent while the others peppered
the newcomer with questions. He watched her slow
and deliberate movements and her precise facial
expressions. She may be new, he thought, and she
may seem different, but so did we when we all met.
He scratched his head and coughed.
"What's your name?" he asked kindly.
The woman turned to him and smiled. "My name is
Elliana. Thank you for asking, Jack."
His mouth fell open in shock but he recovered his
senses a second later. Of course she knew who he
was. He was a famous footballer. He smiled at
Elliana. It's the others that are the weird ones, he
quipped.
The others were not as sharp.
"How," coughed Lesley. "How did you know his...?"
Jack scoffed.
Elliana's appearance had clearly heightened the sense
of trepidation.
"Is," Teddy spoke uneasily. "Is there anyone else
with you?"
Elliana paused before answering. Everything she did
was slow and methodical. It added to her mystique.
"I have come alone," she said.

"And... and you're not lost? You're, I mean, you know what this place is?"

"Yes, Edward, I do."

Teddy stared at her in shock. How could she know his name? He never referred to himself by his proper name. Only one person ever did that.

"Okay, how do you know who we are? You need to give us some answers."

"I don't think so. These issues are not important. You must ask the right questions."

"How are we supposed to know what the *right* questions are?" fumed Wes.

Elliana closed her eyes and sighed softly.

"Begin by asking what you *need* to know, not simply what you *want* to know."

Lesley was confused. "What, and you'll just give us the answers?"

"If they are relevant."

Wes and Teddy shared a look. They were both unsure how to proceed. There were thousands of questions floating in their minds but none would crystallise swiftly enough. Each one clambered for attention and they all drowned each other out. Lesley spoke first.

"Where are we? Where are we going?"

Elliana looked bored, as if she had heard the question many times before. "It doesn't matter. The destination is not important."

"How can it not matter?? We need to know where the hell we are!"

"Why?" countered Elliana.

"Wh-- Well, it..." she stuttered. "We need to know if... if this place is dangerous!"

"It's not."

Wes moaned in frustration. "Look, whoever you are, are you going to give us proper answers?"

Elliana faced the soldier. Her calm demeanour was in stark contrast to his wide-eyed exasperation.

"Are you going to give me proper questions?"

Wes paused, a mixture of anger and confusion etched on his face.

"There are many things I won't tell you," Elliana said. "Mainly because you don't *need* to know them. Other things I can't tell you, because, quite simply, I don't have the answers. But it would probably be a waste of time asking me even if I did.

"I did not create this place," she continued. "I don't own it. I've just been here for a long time. And I have been waiting for you."

The others considered her words carefully.

"So," said Jack slowly. "In your opinion, we don't *need* to know what this place is?"

She nodded curtly.

"Is... Is this a dream? Are we all in a dream?" Elliana stared off into space.

"In a manner of speaking," she replied in her maddeningly enigmatic way.

"Okay, and what do we have to do to... 'wake up'?"

"What have you being doing so far?"

"Walking along this road," said Teddy. "To be honest, we're not even sure if that's the right thing to do. It was all very--"

"Instinctive?" interjected Elliana.

Teddy nodded.

"Good," she said. "Trust your gut. And follow your instincts. That's true in life and it's true here."

"So we're doing the right thing by following the road?" asked Lesley.

"If that is what your heart tells you."

"But you can't give us a straight answer?" said Wes. Elliana rolled her eyes. "Well, you could walk down that way--" she pointed in the direction they had come from, "--or walk across the sand into the abyss. However, you wouldn't get very far. Or rather, strictly speaking, you *would* but you'd be further away from finding your answer."

"What answer?"

"*The* answer. Your denouement. The explanation for everything. All of this."

Teddy thought for a moment. "So, if we stay on the road – and follow it until the end – then we will reach this 'answer'?"

"Yes."

He smirked. "I thought you said the destination wasn't important?"

"It isn't," she said, stifling a sigh. "Don't try to twist my words – it's not going to work.

"The destination is entirely unimportant compared to the journey itself. If you simply appear there then you have cheated yourself out of a vital learning curve and your answer becomes meaningless. This is the same reason I cannot simply tell you what you want to hear."

She looked away from Teddy and studied each one of them.

"When you struggle and suffer and yet still you persevere, you are rewarded in ways you cannot fathom – you will have grown as a person. And at that moment of salvation, far passed the point where you thought you could go on no longer, you realise that the answer, the lesson, you have been chasing this whole time... Well, you knew it all along. Where it once was a worthless piece of knowledge, it now becomes a priceless slice of wisdom."

The group dwelled on her speech in silence for a long time. Elliana moved around freely, stepping off of the road towards the surrounding trees and examining their leaves as if transfixed by their wonders. The sun had moved further across the sky, it still hung high but the day was wearing on. Dusk and darkness would be several hours away, if they came at all in this strange dystopia.

Jack stood up. He had been crouching down, contemplating the situation silently for some time, but he rose with renewed vigour.

"Alright, then," he said brightly. "Shall we get going?"

Wes and Lesley reacted sluggishly. They turned to see how far they had come and wondered how much further there was to go.

"Just a minute, Jack," said Teddy, turning to Elliana. "Okay, why should we trust you? You've not given much indication that you know what's going on here, other than spouting some clichéd rhetoric. Why do we need to follow you?"

Elliana delayed her answer. She turned slowly from the tree she was studying and brought the large leaf back with her as she stepped onto the road. Her hand dropped the leaf and it swung like a melancholy pendulum before coming to rest at her feet.

"You don't," she said simply. "You don't *need* to follow me. You don't *need* to do anything you don't want. That's the whole point. You've been dropped in the middle of nowhere and all you have is your wits – common sense and instinct. Use them. If they tell you to stay here or to follow me then trust them. Don't doubt what you feel is true.

"So, having said that, what do you think?"

She watched Teddy closely. He hesitated while considering his answer. His eyes darted to the side as if looking for assistance from someone.

Eventually Jack spoke.

"I'll be honest. I like her. She's a bit weird. Ah, eh, no offence-- I, I don't get a bad vibe from her. And she seems genuine."

He drew himself up. "I will come with you, Elliana. Or, rather, you can come with us, I'm not really... I'm assuming we're going in the same direction anyway."

Lesley opened her mouth then stopped.

Wes looked at Elliana. He didn't fully trust her, however--

"Hell, me too. I don't trust you, but I'm willing to give you the benefit of the doubt. We're all in this together, right, Lesley?"

He clapped her gently on the shoulder. Lesley smiled in reply then nodded.

Everyone turned to Teddy. He was quiet and, judging by the look on his face, he seemed to be fighting an inner battle.

"Okay, alright," he said at last, avoiding Elliana's eyes. "I think it's a good idea to stay together, especially if you know a little bit about the whole, um, situation. Ah, I... to tell the truth, I don't trust you completely, but I know--"

"It's okay, Teddy," Elliana said kindly. "You don't have to trust me. You only have to trust yourself."

He nodded silently. It took a while to process her words, even longer to formulate a response.

The others smiled and gathered themselves. There was still a long way to go.

The pulsing green emanating from the horizon spilled into the foreground as they walked. Very soon the grass spread out over most of the ground, growing in thick clumps at first and then evolving into fertile thickets that expunged nearly all of the sand. Timid buds cautiously raised their heads among the soft blades and began to slowly open with meticulous care. They quietly refused to be forced by the swift hand of time and approached their task of life with infinitesimal motions. Some lay forever as buds, incubating without ever seeming to grow, others carefully blossomed, waiting patiently for their moment to crown.

Fully bloomed flowers had burst open, spilling their colour and passion into the world. Their delicate petals of pink and purple, red and yellow, flowed from the rich green stem, eager to drink from the sunlight.

Lazy shrubs developed on both sides of the road, with some running together between the flowers to the bases of the trees, which had grown in size and number. Whilst their leaves were plentiful, the sky was still visible through their slender branches.

Much of the newly discovered nature was concentrated around the road. Far off to the sides there were still barren stretches of sterile beige, littered with rocks and warped logs, ignored by time and discarded by life.

Wes looked into the distance off to the side. They had been walking for around half an hour and very few words had been shared. It was much clearer to conclude at this point that following the road was the right thing to do. He glanced across at the expressionless Elliana. She may very well have known that the landscape would become more promising this way, he thought, but it could've been a lucky guess.

Teddy coughed into his hand and laughed spontaneously.

"This is ludicrous," he blurted out into the silence.

Jack chuckled. "What do you mean?"

Teddy turned. His eyes were tired and he looked weary. "All of this. Like, where the hell are we? What is going on? We all bump into each other and suddenly decide to follow this woman who appears out of thin air."

Everyone managed a weak smile and Jack forced another chortle.

"I know, man," he said. "But at least we're moving and, well, it *looks* like we know where we going... in a roundabout sort of way."

"No, no, no, no, Jack. *That's* the crazy part! I mean, sure, we know what to do. But we don't know what we're looking for. Now, isn't that just hilarious..." Teddy trailed off and bowed his head low. He moved with a tired trudge, each step was a laborious task. He barely took any notice of the new surroundings.

Jack was in complete contrast to Teddy. Buoyed by an excitement for adventure, he had pushed any worries to the back of his mind and positively bounced along the road. In moments of prolonged silence, or when someone looked particularly down, Jack would recite words of encouragement in the persona of a football coach:

"Harper, you pick up the pace," he would chide Lesley. "You'll need to work on your fitness if you want to be in my team for Saturday's game. It's a local derby – The Trees vs The Sand. Now drop and give me twenty!"

Lesley strolled in a daze, adrift in her own thoughts, memories, and worries. Awakened from her daydreams only when Jack would spout some good-natured gibberish, she would regularly find herself lagging several metres behind the rest.

She was reliving the recollections she had shared with the others. What really occupied her was the fact she had shared anything at all. And with perfect strangers, too. There was an uneasy comfort between the four of them and that had led Lesley to detail important passages of her life without trepidation. Maybe Teddy was right, she thought. Maybe it *is* easier with strangers because there is no fear of judgement. But Lesley had met plenty of strangers before and not felt compelled to share her life story. It was very hard to think logically here. And Lesley was pulled out of her comfort zone because of it. The quietest person of all was Wes. He marched mechanically onwards in the centre of the road, not trusting Elliana and barely trusting the others. There was an evident unrest that rippled throughout the group, a cold apprehension tinged with weariness and despair. It was an intangible fizzle which defied verbals. So on they slogged in silence.

"Are you okay, Wes?" said Jack jocularly. "You've barely said a word. I'm starting to forget your accent already!"
Wes shot him a swift look of disdain and fixed his eyes ahead.

"Goddamn it, soldier!" exclaimed Jack loudly in a horrid attempt at an American accent. "You answer me when I talk to you, boy!"

Wes exhaled impatiently. "Do us a favour, Jack, and shut it!" he hissed.

Jack stopped and lowered his flailing arms. He recognised that he had gone too far and had antagonised Wes. However, he considered, he had been it doing for a noble reason.

"Come on, Wes, I'm just having a laugh, it's just a joke."

"I know it is. But it's irritating and it makes me want to bury your head in the damn sand!"

Jack sighed. "But there's nobody talking or doing anything. Why do you love silence so much?"

"Why do you *hate* it so much?" Wes shot back.

There was a pause before Jack answered. He looked around at the other four faces. None of them were looking at each other. They were all staring into space.

"Because that's how the demons get in, man."

Suddenly everyone looked at him. His face had dropped its comical grin and he looked a lot more serious.

"I don't mean proper monsters. It's more like, you know... When you're quiet and you keep everything in, you start living your life totally within the confines of your head."

No-one had heard Jack speak so seriously or so eloquently before.

"It's... it's not healthy," he said softly, face to the ground. "You need that balance in life. You don't have to be shouting everything from the rooftops all the time but let a little bit out now and again. I've seen people silently struggle – you can see how much they're suffering – and it tears them apart from the inside."

"Jack..." began Wes.

"I know, I know, I'm sorry. I'm an idiot. I know – I say you don't have to shout from the rooftops and be loud and annoying all the time but... I... I need to do it. Just on occasion. Just every now and then. I have to get it out, because..."

"Because you know what it's like," finished Elliana. "You know what it's like to keep it inside until it eats away at you."

Jack nodded miserably.

"Jesus, Jack, I'm sorry," said Wes.

"It's fine. Really. I know I'm being stupid and annoying. And I know it's not normal here. But the silence--" he covered his face with his hands, "--it just gets to me."

Wes reached out an arm and motioned to pat him on the shoulder. He then changed his mind and placed his hand squarely on Jack's bowed head.

"Do you want to talk about it?" he asked.

Jack shook his head.

"Are you sure?" said Lesley. "It's very therapeutic."

Jack did not react.

Teddy tried a different tact. "How did you get into socc-- Er, football? I'm really curious as to how someone can climb the ladder up to world class level..."

He left the proposition hanging in the air. Jack looked up and smiled weakly.

"I know what you're trying to do," he said.

Teddy threw his arms up innocently. Then Lesley screamed. "You tell us your bloody story or you'll be running laps of this goddamn desert until your shoes wear away!!"

Everyone laughed and the tension eased. They all turned to walk again. Jack ran a hand through his hair and cleared his throat.

Chapter Seven

"I'm not really sure how to start. I guess I'll just go from what I can remember...

"My first memory is catching a football. Well, sort of catching it. The ball flew over to me and I had my arms up in the air. It slipped right through them and slapped me square in the face. I can't remember where it was, some local club but there was quite a big crowd. Most people seemed to enjoy talking to each other as much as actually watching the game. But I was transfixed by this match. The size of these players, the skill they had. They could manipulate the ball with their feet so intricately and extravagantly that people called it art. I suppose I still think of it that way, almost twenty years later.

"The guy who had sent the ball looping in my direction came across with a smile on his face. He asked me if I was alright and messed up my hair. Then he promised I could come on the pitch at half time and take a penalty. I was so happy. To be honest, I don't remember going on the field. My dad says I fell over the first time and the whole crowd cheered. Then they let me take the shot again and I scored. I was allowed to take the ball home and, for the few months I had it before it was completely worn away, it was my prized possession... In hindsight, that's probably the day it all began."

It was actually Jack's neighbour, old Mrs Corbett, who originally forced him into playing for a local team. Finally fed up of the rhythmic thumping of footballs against her wall, she implored Jack's parents to sign him up for a boys' club. His new manager could hardly believe his eyes as he watched Jack slalom nonchalantly through the opposition players time and again in his first match. At half time, his eyes nearly popped out of his head when he noticed the eight year old Jack juggling the ball expertly with his feet for the full ten minute break.

It became clear over the next few years that Jack's sublime talent was matched only by his coolness on the pitch. There was no opponent too daunting and no crowd too big for him. Every week, he had ice in his veins as soon as he crossed the white line. Despite his calm exterior, Jack was as passionate about the game as anyone else. He celebrated the victories with reckless exuberance and felt the losses more keenly than his teammates. His passion and commitment, not to mention his talent, set him apart.

It wasn't long before the big teams came knocking. On the last day of a topsy-turvy season, Jack's team required a win to clinch the league title. A savage gale blew across the park and a bitter chill descended and refused to budge. His teammates were timid as they took to the field but the fifteen year old Jack didn't let a small detail like that detract from his performance.

It was a remarkable game, more akin to a brutal battle than a football match. Three times Jack had dragged his team back into contention with moments of impudent brilliance. Caked in mud, covered in bruises and half-exhausted, he watched helplessly as the opposition broke away in the dying seconds: the striker mishit the shot, it swerved to the goalkeeper's far left, struck a divot, and looped over the despairing defender on the line. With an apologetic glance behind, the ball guiltily nestled itself in the corner of the goal.

Jack did not need to hear the referee's shrill final whistle seconds later to know it was all over. His limbs seemed to go numb and, without fully understanding how he got there, he sat alone in the dressing room, unable to conjure up any more fight to stop the tears streaming relentlessly down his face. Time passed slowly and yet all at once.

After an eternity the door opened and Jack's father walked in. He sat silently next to him for several minutes and let him cry.

"It's not fair," mumbled Jack tonelessly.

His father smiled. "I know, son. But that's football. It's why you love the game."

"I hate it."

"I know you do. And you feel terrible now. You will for a while. But don't forget, it's a good thing."

Jack sniffed. "How can this be good?"

His father placed his hand on his shoulder. "The only thing that can hurt you this deeply is something you love, something you allow to live that close to your heart. Great pain comes from great affection. That's how you know you will heal, and become even stronger for having suffered."

Eventually Jack raised his head. His eyes were puffy and red and tinged with tears. It was then that he realised there was another man in the dressing room too, hovering near the door. He had followed Jack's dad inside and stood quietly the whole time.

"Jack, this is Noah Harris."

The man smiled warmly. Jack stared at him blankly.

"Noah is a scout. He... he works for Manchester United."

"Hello, Jack," Noah said. He had light brown eyes and a kind face.

Jack's eye widened in shock. He looked at the long black jacket Noah was wearing and noticed the large red badge of his own boyhood idols. His dad beamed at him.

Noah came forward and sat on the bench opposite. He spoke softly, mentioning the game, Jack's performance, a little about Manchester United, arrangements for a trial, more information...

Jack hardly took anything in. He was still in shock. The sadness inside him had evaporated and was replaced with frenzied excitement, slowly bubbling up, fuelling his imagination with visions of stadiums, state of the art facilities, fame, and fortune.

"The first few years there were amazing. I had everything I could possibly want – training pitches, an incredible gym, healthy meals, access to everything. And, of course, world class coaching. The people were amazing, every single one of them. I felt immediately at home. For the first three years, until I was about nineteen, I spent half my time at the training centre, constantly working and improving, listening to advice. I broke into the first team around that time and then I suppose I let my work ethic slide a little. I was still doing as much work as, if not more than, everyone else. But when I made it into the squad, I started to get a lot more money. And I wanted to enjoy spending it.

"Everyone goes a bit crazy with their first real pay. I was no different, I just... Well, I just got a lot more than most people my age get. So I bought the fancy car and the nice flat overlooking the water. And I would go out and enjoy the night life the rest of the time. There were a few of us around the same age and we did what young people do. Stupid stuff, nothing dangerous. Although, yeah, we probably took it a little too far on occasion. It was always like that. For a while it was just 'work hard, play hard.' We were given a little leeway by the manager because we still delivered the results on a Saturday. And then one day, when I was twenty three, I woke up and everything... everything changed."

Jack wearily opened his eyes. Everything was blurry. Was the room spinning? He blinked hard and opened them again. It was his head - his head was spinning and his eyes tried and failed to focus. It took a minute or two for him to gain his bearings. With an almighty effort he raised his head (resting against something rough and... leathery?) and looked around.
The view was obstructed by the bed he had clearly fallen out of at some point in the night. He found himself lying on the floor, fully clothed. His head had been resting on an old football boot.

There was a dull and muffled humming noise, intermittently sounding from somewhere near his feet. He sat up slowly, his whole body fighting against the movement, and looked below the portion of his thick duvet that covered his phone. The screen was illuminated and Jack could just about make out the telephone symbol and the word "Gaffer" on it. With a jolt, he fully awoke. He jumped up and assessed the mess in his room. It was in a terrible state – several empty beer bottles were dotted around and at least one had smashed on the floor. Indeterminate foodstuffs were scattered haphazardly, having fallen from one of many white containers on the desk. The large, red curtain was askew, having been ripped from its fastenings in the corner. Blinding sunlight streamed in through the window.

Jack sat on the edge of his bed after surveying the damage. He remained still for a long time, ignoring his phone, miserably trying to piece together the events from the previous night. This was far from the first time he had woken up wretched and hungover, but, as he sat there, despondent, with his head in his hands, it felt different. There was a deep-seated uneasiness within him, lingering beneath and beyond the physical pain he was experiencing. Something wasn't right.

The rest of that lonely Monday Jack spent in his flat, repairing the damage he had drunkenly caused. He had not touched his phone and felt a horrible pang of guilt when he thought about it. In the cold, dreary afternoon, he watched the rain pound the pavements on the street below. He had spent a long time in the bath trying to make sense of the foreboding he felt, and now, as he sat by the window, absorbing the monotonous grey of the colourless world, the melancholy overwhelmed him.

For hours Jack wept, feeling more lonely at this point than at any other in his life. He curled up on the chair and glanced towards the television. One of his favourite comedies was on, but it washed over him and he took nothing in. His headache had subsided and the queasiness was all but gone, and yet he still felt horrible.

He woke early the next day and arrived at the training centre not long after dawn. He did not expect anyone to be in but if he was to speak to the manager then he preferred it that way. He could not face the other players today. As he drove into the car park, he noticed the manager's car was already there. A thin layer of frost lay upon the windscreen – the boss had been here for a while.

Jack took a deep breath and walked along the corridor to the office. The door was lying open. That was strange. The boss operated an open-door policy but it was never taken literally. Jack paused when he reached the doorway. He took a deep breath, mentally organising his thou--

"Come on in, Jack."

The voice of his manager drifted out into the corridor. Jack hesitantly stepped forward into the room. He had expected anger and curses flung relentlessly in his direction but instead his manager was sitting behind his desk with a comforting smile on his face. He stood when Jack entered and placed two steaming mugs on his desk.

"Take a seat. Oh, and close the door, would you?"

Jack obliged, still surprised at the courteous welcome. He must be warming up for a bollocking, he thought.

"Have a cup of tea."

"Tea?"

"Yes, you'll feel better after it."

Jack sipped and felt the warmth radiate through him at once. He looked up and saw his manager surveying him closely.

"How are you doing, Jack?"

"I'm fine," came the dull reply.

"No you're not."

Jack looked out of the window. The light was still pale and barely illuminated the grey car park. Dark puddles remained from the rain the day before. In the distance he could just make out the training pitches through the thin mist. Normally, he was desperate to be out there but now it was the last place in the world he wanted to be. He swallowed nervously.

"I... I'm sorry I wasn't at training yesterday. I was... I didn't feel well."

He bowed his head and waited for the response. When it didn't come he looked up.

"I know you were hungover. And I know you ignored my phone calls."

He looked sternly at Jack and paused before continuing.

"But I don't care about that," he said, waving an arm.

Jack squirmed anxiously. If the gaffer no longer cared about him then he was, at best, out of the team, and, at worst, surely heading for the exit.

"However, I am disappointed in you. You've not been well for a while now, Jack. You are the loudest person I know. I hear you long before I see you. Echoing down the corridors like some kind of demented foghorn. And you're great with the other players, too, always talking, giving encouragement and criticism when it's needed. Your attitude and personality is more important to this club than your footballing talent."

He clasped his hands together and rested his chin on them.

"But you've slowly retreated within yourself recently. I could tell you were going through something. I could tell you were suffering. And I'm disappointed you never came to me about it. It's not just about the football here. I would sacrifice any number of games for your health and wellbeing."

Jack's bottom lip trembled. It was true. He had not been well for a while now. He had assumed it was a virus, the 'flu, maybe the cold, or even the hangovers. But now that he thought about it, something hadn't felt right for a long time.

"I didn't know..." he said. "Why didn't you say something to me, boss?"

"Because it's a massive step when you realise it yourself, like you did yesterday. That way, you are aware of the problem and the process is then fully under your control. If someone tells you that you're not well, you could easily deny it. Even to yourself. And denial is dangerously unhealthy.

"Please understand, I wouldn't have let it go on forever, Jack. But I am glad you came to me when you did."

"I..." Jack began after a pause. "I didn't come to... I only came to explain why I wasn't at training yesterday."

"Maybe that's what you decided at first. But then ask yourself: why did you come at a time you knew it would be empty around here?"

Jack shrugged. He sipped his tea and thought back to the night before. He had lain awake for hours, unable to sleep. At some point he had resolved to come in early, before the crowds, and see the manager to explain himself. But he had other reasons for coming in. He wasn't sure exactly what they were. At the very least he wanted to clear the air.

"So, what do I do now?" asked Jack. "Should I train now I'm here?"

"Do you want to?"

Jack hesitated and, before he could reply, his manager spoke.

"I don't want you to train today. In fact, take the week off. Go home, see your family, and forget about football for a few days. Take as much time as you need. Just let me know how you're doing and when you're ready to come back."

The manager watched as Jack fidgeted with his mug.

"But we've got a game on Saturday, boss."

"Yes, but you won't be playing. I'm not giving you the added pressure of performing in front of seventy thousand people. All you have to focus on is getting better."

At that moment Jack felt a great weight release from his chest. His breathing, at once, felt less constricted and he smiled for what felt like the first time in weeks. He took another gulp of tea.

"What about my teammates? Will they not be angry? And the press? What are you going to tell them?"

"I'll take care of that. It's none of your concern."

"But," Jack did not fully understand. "How can you give me time off just because I'm a bit down? It--"

"When was the last time you spoke to Marcus?"

Jack was caught off guard by the abrupt change in subject.

"Marcus?" he asked, thinking of his teammate who had been injured for several months. Jack considered him his closest friend.

"Yes. When was the last time you spoke?"

"I dunno. Well, I send him a few texts every week but I've not seen him for a while now. I think he's really busy with his recovery."

"Jack, Marcus isn't injured. We told everyone, including his teammates and the press, that he had hurt his ankle ligaments. People get injured all the time so nobody raised any questions and it's never been an issue."

"Well, where is he?" Jack asked, confused.

"He's been back home in London for nearly four weeks now, spending time with his family, taking a break from the pressure here.

"Jack, Marcus has been suffering from depression. For a long time. He's been dealing with it through the use of anti-depressants and by visiting a therapist."

Jack was shocked. Not only by the revelation but because Marcus had never even broached the subject with him.

"Just under a couple of years ago he acted in a similar way to how you have been acting recently. He was much more quiet. He was more within himself. And this was unlike the player, or the person, that both of us have known him to be in the past."

Jack nodded. He and Marcus had been best friends immediately when they arrived at the youth academy. Marcus was a year older and broke into the first team a week before Jack. They had even shared a flat together for a year. He now recalled the period after they moved into their separate accommodations. Marcus had been in his shell a little more and Jack had teased that it was because he was missing his old roommate so much.

"I gave him some time off and recommended he speak to a professional. Eventually, he returned to his normal self, although he has been on anti-depressants ever since. Well, until last month. He came in, as early as you did today, and we chatted for a long time. He was making the decision to stop taking his medication and asked for some time off to adjust."

"And you let him?"

"Of course, Jack. Like I said, the health and wellbeing of the people here is more important than the results on a Saturday. I've been keeping in contact with him and he says that, after a shaky week or so, he has begun to cope very well. He may return soon, although I won't rush him back."

Jack looked out of the window again and thought about his manager's words. The sun had crept higher over the trees and illuminated the ground below. A car pulled up in the car park and Olive, one of the chefs, stepped out. She tugged her hood over her head and strolled briskly towards the entrance off to the right.

"Are you sure you should be telling me about Marcus, boss?"

"It was his idea. Marcus is not ashamed of his condition, Jack. He is aware there is still an unfortunate stigma attached to some mental illnesses – although it is very, very slight now – and he suggested that, whilst he is happy for people to know the truth, it may be easier to a attribute his absence to a minor injury. No, I don't think he will have a problem with me telling you this."

The two of them sat in silence for a while. Eventually, when other staff members began to arrive, Jack stood up to leave.

"Before you go, son, take this."

He handed Jack a card with the number of a therapist on it.

"I would like you to speak to someone. Seeing a psychiatrist may not be for you, but please give it a go. It does a lot of good to open up now and again. Try not to keep things bottled up. And please recognise when you need to ask for help."

Jack thanked him. He set his empty mug back on the desk and headed towards the door.

"Remember, I have an open-door policy, Jack," his manager said. "Never be afraid to come to me with any issues."

Jack nodded and smiled. "Got it, boss."

"Good. Please close the door behind you."

Chapter Eight

Jack trailed off into silence. The others walked quietly alongside him. Eventually Elliana spoke.

"We all have our battles. Even the ones that seem the happiest can be at war within themselves. In fact, it is often these people that suffer the most."

Lesley's gaze lingered on her for a second before switching back to the footballer.

"So what did you end up doing?" she asked. "Did you meet up with your friend?"

"Oh, yeah." Jack said. "How could I not, after hearing what he was going through? It's crazy..."

He stopped for a second and looked off into the distance. His hands covered his face then fell limply to his sides.

"You know," he continued. "I never had a clue. Not at all. It's amazing how he kept it hidden for so long. You're right, Elliana, it is people like Marcus who can be the most vulnerable; they spend so much of their time focused on others that they forget about themselves.

"After that meeting, I rang Marcus from the car. But, before the call even connected, I hung up. I decided I should go down and visit him. I didn't think twice about it even though it was a good few hours' drive. When I got there, his jaw nearly hit the floor. I was a little hesitant when I was hovering at the doorway but the look on his face...

"We ended up chatted for ages – I couldn't believe it had been so long since we spoke last. And it was like the last three or four years just... melted away and we were two eighteen year olds laughing about stupid things, dreaming about taking on the world. I ended up staying for hours."

"Did you talk about his... About how he was doing, recovery-wise?"

"Eventually. We're not exactly the most open of people (show me a young man that is!) but we got around to it. I sort of delayed it because he kept asking why I wasn't at training and I fobbed him off a couple of times. But, yeah, we got around to it. I told him my head wasn't in the right place and the gaffer was giving me a few days off and I think he knew what was going on right then and there, just by my demeanour, really. Then I told him, pretty bluntly I guess, that I knew why he wasn't at training either. That the boss had told me everything. I was pretty nervous because I didn't know what sort of reaction to expect. His face was still for a second then he just broke into a proper ear-to-ear smile. You could tell how relieved he was."

Jack smiled at the memory. He looked down at the ground and cleared his throat.

"It was like having my friend back, you know. And it wasn't an uncomfortable issue to talk about. It just became another topic of conversation like football, girls, the TV schedule..."

"What about after that? Did you go back to football?" asked Teddy after a long pause.

"Oh, yeah," Jack nodded, turning to look at him. "Together."

Wes smiled and clapped him on the back. "You're a great guy, Jack. Your friend's lucky to have you."

"Thanks, but I'm the lucky one. Marcus is more important – he's the better guy. And he had the tougher battle. You know, he's the better friend. Just like Elliana was saying."

Elliana had her head turned upwards and was serenely studying the sky.

"I wasn't talking about Marcus," she said softly.

"What? You mean... You meant me?" Jack blinked dumbly.

Elliana nodded in reply, her gaze still focused away from the group.

Lesley agreed. "Yes, that's the whole impression I got as well."

Jack laughed nervously. "You're... you're joking, right? That's... I don't think you were listening to the story."

"Think about it," Teddy said. "Other than ignoring your manager's phone calls that day, none of the story really casts you in a bad light. Of course, you may be biased but the way you told it seemed genuine. And you are very hard on yourself. At least, that is the impression I got from it."

Wes nodded in agreement and smiled at Jack, whose brow was furrowed in thought.

"If you cast your mind back to your meeting," said Elliana, "and you think carefully, you will recall the moment the pressure on you seemed to ease. You put this down to being granted a break from your professional duties, as if that was the relief you needed. However, maybe your memory is a little hazy? My view is that you immediately felt better upon hearing your close friend was suffering. At that moment, your own concern for yourself evaporated and you identified helping Marcus as your priority." Lesley smiled warmly at Jack and laid a hand on his arm. "You know, I think she's right."

"Well... I suppose..." the footballer stuttered.

"How did your own recovery progress beyond that point?" pressed Teddy.

"Er, well, I spoke to therapist, I saw her a few times, twice a week at first then just once a week for the last few months. She said I didn't particularly need any medication unless I wanted it because I seemed healthy and vibrant. Just not healthy enough to stop seeing her. Then again, she was getting paid for her time."

"I would imagine that, after a period of time, it would be your own decision to discontinue the sessions. How long ago did you start seeing her?" He waved his arm at the surroundings and added: "Well, relatively speaking."

"Six or seven months. To be honest, I think it just helps to have someone to talk to. It's not even about healing or treating an illness for me. It's about having an outlet. In fact, now that I think about it, I probably chat more with Marcus than with my therapist. It helps when someone has been down the same road as you."

"Yes, it does," remarked Wes, his gaze fixed firmly on Elliana.

The sun had finally dipped in the sky. It still beamed powerfully but the heat was less punishing and the shadows on the ground were longer. Modicums of dust gently hovered in the wake of each footstep, swirling hopefully in the presence of movement but reluctantly returning to the ceaseless and sterile road. In many ways the road *was* sterile – blank, grey, devoid of curve and character, pulling off endlessly towards the stoic horizon. The individual intuition of the group, however, suggested the path was the only morsel of hope in an otherwise barren land.

"Can you give us any more answers yet?" Lesley asked Elliana for what felt like the tenth time.

"That depends," answered Elliana for what felt like the twentieth. "Can you give me any more relevant questions yet?"

Wes turned his head away and gritted his teeth in frustration.

"How about *your* story?" Jack said. "How did you get here? And what did you do before?"

There was a flicker of annoyance on Elliana's face as she glanced towards him and then off into the distance again.

"That's not important. And it wouldn't help you."

Jack let out a long, toneless whistle. It echoed off the surrounding trees.

"Why," began Teddy, "is it so important for us to discover the answers ourselves? Why can't you tell us what we need to hear and make sure we understand it so we can leave?"

"Come on, you know why. It doesn't work like that in the real world so why would it work here?"

"A-ha!" exclaimed Teddy. "So you're saying this *isn't* the real world?!"

She stared at him blankly for a second and then turned away. "You are quite clearly not asking the right questions."

"I'm pretty sure it was just a figure of speech," Lesley whispered to an exasperated Teddy.

She then turned to Elliana. "What are the *right* questions then? Can't you give us any advice?"

Elliana pondered for a moment.

"As I have already said – you brought yourselves here. There is a way you can leave, but it is entirely up to you to find it. Only you can get yourself out."

"Okay, we're not children," replied Teddy. "We don't need to be mollycoddled. We're adults and deserve to be treated as such."

"Quite," said Elliana. "Then perhaps you will recognise what you need to do instead of pestering me for answers you know you will not receive."

"Right, okay, guys," said Jack. "She's only trying to help so--"

"Is she, though?" interjected Wes.

"Yes. I think so. I believe so. For argument's sake, at least, let's assume she *is* trying to help us."

The others reluctantly fell silent.

"Alright, then," Jack went on. "I just think we should maybe give her a break. Cut her some slack, you know," he said, then turned to Elliana. "Look, we're all pretty messed up, we're lost, we're irritable, we don't know how to get home. Please, if you can, give us some help, some indication of what we are supposed to be doing."

Elliana looked at him for a long time then quickly switched her gaze to the others. "I appreciate your situation. I'm sorry, I know you're upset and nervous, but there's just very little I can do. I am bound by rules that forb--"

"But who gave you these rules?" Jack cut in.

"I'm sorry, really I am, but I can't tell you," she said as the others sighed. "I can't give you the answers. I can only show you where to look."

A minute or two passed before anyone spoke.

"So what do you suggest we do?" asked Lesley.

Elliana almost shrugged her shoulders. "We continue walking."

Everyone filed in behind her, feeling a little more dejected and a little more hopeless. Their nerves were building and their patience was fraying.

"Okay, I've been thinking," said Jack at last. "Maybe there is a real, physical answer at the end of this road, like a door and a key, or maybe there's a... baddie... we need to fight, I don't know. But my opinion is that, as we agreed, this is all probably a dream. And we are obviously here to deal with any issues we have. I don't know, but maybe we should be talking, opening up and sharing our stories, like we have been doing."

"Sounds a bit far-fetched," Wes said pointedly. "Besides, not everyone has shared their story so far."

"Well, *I* don't think it's necessary that people know the ins and outs of *my* life," said Teddy quickly.

"Um, I was actually talking about her," he pointed to Elliana.

"Oh, sorry," said Teddy sheepishly.

"It's maybe not vital for everyone to tell their whole life story," Jack said awkwardly. "Perhaps that's not why we're here. Er... I was just thinking that the reason we're here could have something to do with past decisions. You know, like 'what's your biggest regret?' and 'what's your biggest fear?' Maybe we've been brought here because we're supposed to change something about our lives."

Wes raised a sceptical eyebrow.

Lesley nodded. "I don't see why not. I have no idea if that's the real reason, but since it doesn't look like we'll get any real answers, it could be worth a shot. Teddy?"

"I don't know," Teddy hesitated. "It might be a good way to pass the time but I don't see how answering some questions will unlock a secret doorway for us to get home or how it's going to make me wake up in my office again."

"Why not?" asked Jack. "You woke up here."

"Okay, then," Teddy said coolly. "Why don't you start? What's your biggest fear?"

"Probably that we'll never get out of here," Jack remarked.

Teddy laughed.

"Er, I dunno," said Jack. "I... try not to think about it. Maybe I shouldn't go first."

"It's fine, Jack, really. Take your time," said Lesley. Jack cleared his throat. He thought for a while before starting hesitantly.

"I'd probably say... fading away. I know that's a pretty obvious answer for someone like me who is famous for doing something I love. But I have this fear that I'll be forgotten, like I'll be usurped. Don't get me wrong, if someone is a better player than me then I'll admit it, but it's that nagging feeling that I've been..."

He trailed off and thought for a moment. Eventually he started.

"Do you know what it is? D'you know what it feels like? I feel... I feel like a fraud."

"A fraud?"

"Yep. Like I only made it by accident and there's no real basis to my career other than luck. I dunno, it probably doesn't make sense."

Teddy was nodding. "No, it makes sense. I understand. The reason you feel that way is because it's true."

Jack looked up in shock.

"Teddy!" Lesley exclaimed.

"Let me finish! I don't mean you're not good enough or even that you don't deserve it. Evidently you belong at the level you play at (I assume, of course, because I've never seen you play.) But that voice in the back of your mind – that feeling that you're a fraud – it's totally natural especially in a field as fluid and unscientific as sports. You've had enormous amounts of luck – you would be the first to admit this. And you are surely aware of other players of comparable skill to you that didn't quite 'make it.' So you probably thinking you're a fraud because there's other people out there who didn't get the breaks that you did.

"But that doesn't mean you don't deserve your luck." Jack listened carefully but was not fully convinced.

"Let me ask you this," Teddy went on. "What did you do for the first three or four years after you signed for Manchester United?"

"Er, not much. I trained a lot and spent a lot of time at the gym. I didn't really do much else."

"Exactly, Jack! You worked hard. You put effort into realising your dream. You may have had the luck to get you to that position but you sure as hell didn't take it for granted. Some people have the talent and the skill but don't make it. That's their tragedy. Not yours.

"Of course, you could get involved with organisations to help these people. To minimise the number of people who don't get that luck they need. Not just in football, but in any professional sector. And, if anyone is selfless enough to give their time and energy to such a venture, it's you, Jack."

Jack scratched his head thoughtfully.

"Oh, and as for the fading away part," Teddy said. "For one thing, you're in your early twenties so it's only natural to consider your existence and worry about the world. But maybe your fear of disappearing is linked to your career after football. It's probably all an unknown to you. You might retire when you're thirty five or forty and have plenty of money to fall back on, or you could get injured next week and your career ends on the spot. It sounds scary, I know, but don't worry about it. Have a think about what your other interests are and start planning ahead. Talk to friends and family. Live in the moment but plan for the future."

He watched as Jack slowly nodded.

"You're right. God, you're right. That does make sense. Man, you're good at this."

Teddy blushed slightly then looked pointedly at the ground. "Oh, dear, that's a shame – no magic doorway!"

"If you don't mind me asking," said Wes. "Do you have any big regrets? I know you've had a lot of luck but do you ever wish it had turned out differently?"

"Not really," said Jack. "I'm glad I realised early on how lucky I was. I wish I'd spent more time talking with Marcus, obviously, when we were younger. And the others like him. I've known a few people who have drifted away and I wish I had kept in contact with them. But other than that, it's just little things – I wish I'd enjoyed being younger a lot more."

"What about going out? When you were drinking and acting stupid? Do you wish you could take that back?"

"Do you know what?" Jack said after a pause. "I barely touch alcohol now. And I did some really stupid stuff when I was younger – there's memories I still cringe at. But no, I don't regret it. Not one second of it. I miss those days but I don't want to relive them. They were... It's like they were of their time. Also, if you can't be stupid when you're young then when can you be?"

Wes nodded approvingly. "I like that attitude. It's good... To be honest, I'm probably the same. If anything, I wish I had gone out and acted stupid even more than I did. But it's easy to say that now. If I was to go back, there's no way I would sacrifice time with my dad to hang out with my friends for a year or two."

"Did you cut yourself off from your friends?" asked Lesley.

"No," Wes shook his head. "I had – have – great friends from my home town. They knew how important my family was to me, but I didn't isolate myself from my friends in favour of my dad. It wasn't like that, if that's what you're asking. They would all come round to the house, just pop their heads in whenever they liked. My parents loved it. I've always thought they wanted more kids, actually, so they liked the place being full of noise and happiness."

He smiled at the memories. The whoops and shouts came flooding back to him, echoing around the kitchen whilst his mother tried to cook. The room was a mess and there was flour in her hair. But it did not stop her laughing along with everyone else.

"What are you afraid of?" Jack asked. "What's your biggest fear?"

It took Wes a long time to answer.

"I loved those times. I loved growing up. I know not everyone does but I never had to worry about anything because dad would fix it. It was always like that. And after he was gone there were some tough years. So obviously that was my biggest fear originally, and it came true. I think I'm still healing from it. But I choose to remember the good times." He sighed deeply before continuing.

"I guess the thing I fear most is not being able to relive those times. Or, rather, recreate those times. Every time I think of being young, I remember the happiness. And... What if I never have that again? What if the best days of my life have already passed me by?"

He let his words linger in the air. It was the first time he had vocalised these feelings and, quite possibly, the first time he had recognised they existed.

His reverie was interrupted by Teddy.

"Well, that's ridiculous."

"What's so ridiculous about it?" said Jack.

"Well, the fear itself is probably universal. The fear of the future or the unknown. Everyone worries about it. But it's ludicrous."

"Why?"

"Because there's nothing you can do about it. The future will come. Whether it's good or bad. And the only influence we have on it are the decisions we make in the present. Look, Wes," he turned to the soldier. "You can choose to be afraid. You can choose to believe that all happiness is behind you. But that is a painful and lonely path. As long as your trust yourself and remember the lessons your father taught you, there will be plenty of joy in your future. Sometimes you just have to create the happiness yourself."

Wes listened with his head bowed. "I understand. But I still worry. I've seen people do bad things, terrible things. And, from time to time, I find it very hard to trust that we live in a good place. What if everything falls apart?"

"Oh, I wouldn't worry about it," said Elliana. "There's far too much beauty in the world for that." Wes looked up at her. She was still staring at the sky and seemed detached from the rest of them but was evidently listening intently.

"How do you mean?" Lesley asked.

Elliana turned to look at Wes and smiled.

"Look at the four of you, for example. Four strangers, waking in a strange land where there are no rules and no signposts. And what do you do? You decide to trust each other.

"The kindness of humanity cannot be overstated. And it must never be forgotten."

Wes half-returned the smile then looked away. It was as if Elliana had never seen the real world. There was peace and beauty, sure, but there was also heartbreak, destruction, and sadness.

"Well, I guess you all know my worst fear," Lesley spoke into the silence. "What if I don't help enough people? What if I don't do my part? I don't know what that would do to me."

"You can only do what you can, Lesley," said Jack. "You might not be able to change the whole world but you can change-- what was it that woman told you? You can show kindness and compassion to people who will then do the same and, one day, when the chain continues, they will move mountains."

"I know, and that's true, but I've not helped a single soul yet. And that's not going to change if I stay at my job. I don't even know why I'm there!"

"Then quit. Or, at least, be prepared to if it's costing you your happiness. Frankly, I don't see why you're the secretary in an office when you could be the secretary for a shelter somewhere. Or for some voluntary organisation. Or, why the hell not, running your own orphanage?"

Lesley was taken aback.

"Yes, why not?" chimed in Teddy. "You have the passion, you have personal experience of growing up in that environment so you could mould it in your own style. *And* you have the professional experience of working in an office which would definitely be useful when you're setting up – you could do it!"

"You could totally do it, Lesley" smiled Wes.

Lesley stared at each of their beaming faces, tears slowly welling in her eyes.

"Well, yes... I suppose it's possible..." she murmured.

"Of course it is," said Jack, squeezing her on the shoulder. "Think about it. Think about how you can make a difference."

"But don't think it to death," said Wes. "At some point, you're going to have to take a deep breath and jump in."

"And you say you've never helped anyone," Teddy said. "Well, that's ridiculous. You've helped all of us, by listening, talking, advising... just by your presence, really. You're a very pleasant person to be around."

"Thank you, Teddy, that's lovely of you to say, but I've not helped you. I don't know anything about you. You haven't told us your story, your hopes or your fears."

"Oh, that's alright, you don't need to worry about me," he replied uneasily.

"Why not?"

"I speak to people every day. I've seen people suffer and know the steps they need to take to recover."

"Surely the people speak to you?" asked Jack. "You don't get to tell them your problems."

"Because I don't need to, believe me. I'm very lucky that I found what I love to do at an early age and I've never really had many of the problems that my patients seem to face."

Wes watched Teddy as he walked. His shoulders were tucked in and his head was inclined downwards. Wes noticed the lines on his face and felt he could occasionally glimpse the weariness in his brown eyes.

"What do you do?" Wes asked him.

Teddy blinked. "I... I'm a psychiatrist, haven't I said?"

"Yes, I mean, apart from that. Other than work, what do you do?"

"I... I like to think I'm always working in some way. It is not a simple nine-to-five job when you're dealing closely with people."

"Okay then. Your free time. What do you do?"

Teddy stared at him coldly. "Why?"

"I'm just curious."

"Well, I enjoy reading," said Teddy bitterly. "And long walks through the forest nearby my house."

Wes nodded and attempted a warm smile.

"Are you married?"

Teddy looked away. "It's none of your goddamn business."

He turned away and continued walking.

After several minutes of awkward silence Jack cleared his throat and called Elliana's name.

"So how long have you been here then?" he asked.

"Some time," came the response.

"Before us? Did you know who we were? How did you know where we were?"

She did not reply.

"Alright, any chance you want to tell us your worst fear, biggest regret? No?"

Wes cut across him. "Look, Teddy, I'm sorry, I didn't mean to offend you, I was just asking questions."

"Yeah," nodded Lesley. "We just want you to open up."

"Why?!" Teddy hissed. "Because you've all done it and now your lives are sorted? Or is it to appease this maniac here?" He gestured to Elliana. "She doesn't know what's going on, and we're mad to trust her."

Elliana made a slight movement although her expression remained the same.

"Look, everyone," continued Teddy. "I'm not doing this because I don't like her – although I've not hidden that – but we need to look at the facts here. She has just appeared out of nowhere – the same as us! – and just expects us to follow her? She won't give us any answers. Nothing she says makes any sense--"

"Well, hang on," interjected Jack. "Just because you don't understand her, it doesn't mean she's evil or trying to harm us."

"She's already harmed us by dumping us in this hellhole!" Teddy shot back.

"I'm just saying we should give her a chance--"

"Teddy's right," said Wes. "I'm not saying she's the one that brought us here or that she means us any harm, but she's the number one suspect right now. And we deserve answers."

Jack opened his mouth to argue. He turned to Lesley who was avoiding his gaze.

"I'm not saying we should condemn her, Jack, but don't you agree we are entitled to the truth?"

Elliana had resolutely continued walking while the others discussed her although Jack could see her eyes darting to both sides and a red tinge to her cheeks. His voice wavered as he called her name again.

"Yes, Jack?" replied Elliana. Her voice was slightly higher than normal.

"What, er, what do you think we should do? We've been here for hours, and you are the only person who knows what's going on... So, c-could you tell us more, please? Can give us the answers?"

There was a brief silence that seemed to stretch for hours.

"Some time today, please!" said Wes.

"Come on," Teddy prompted shrilly.

"We should continue walking," she said at last.

Both Wes and Lesley groaned while Jack sighed miserably.

"No!" Teddy growled and almost galloped forwards to confront her.

At the sound of his voice Elliana turned, startled. As she spun on the spot, she lost her footing and stumbled backwards. By the time she had composed herself, Teddy was in front of her face.

"I've had enough," he yelled. "Tell us what's happening! Who are you? What the hell is going on?!"

There was a dull crack of thunder somewhere above them. The wind howled menacingly.

Elliana's eyebrows arched angrily and her gaze flickered to the other three standing several feet behind.

"You have to be patient and be prep--"

"To hell with this!" shouted Wes. "This is crazy! Who the hell do you think you are? Giving us orders like you're in charge? You're a fraud and a liar."

Elliana stuttered as she tried to speak. "Lesley, Jack, surely you--"

But Jack put his hands up. "I'm sorry but you need to answer some questions."

"They're right," said Lesley, her eyes swimming with tears. "Because we're desperate now. And we're scared."

Elliana opened her mouth and closed it again as questions were fired at her.

"Who are you?"

"Why are you here?"

"Why should we listen to you?!"

Wes folded his arms menacingly.

Teddy spat into the dust at their feet.

Lesley watched as Elliana squirmed under the questions. Her head was bowed and Lesley saw a tear fall to the ground.

When Elliana lifted her head, her face was a picture of beautiful agony. She looked much younger. Tears flowed down her cheeks and her bottom lip quivered.

Jack took a step towards her, gently touched her arm and looked into her eyes, blue into blue.

"Elliana," he said softly. "What's going on?"

She could sense the others forming a semi-circle around her but her eyes never left Jack's.

The wind, which had slowly rumbled and grown louder, now dissipated into silence and the leaves that had been swirling in the air around them now fell gracefully to the ground.

Elliana looked at the others then lowered her gaze and then whispered the words that chilled their bones.

"I'm lost too!"

Chapter Nine

Long shadows stretched along the landscape as the sun edged closer towards the horizon. There was a slow, mournful breeze gently rolling along the ground and tumbling through the trees. Other than the soft whistle of the wind, there was silence.

At long last someone spoke.

"How," said Wes. "How the *hell* can this be happening?!"

He sounded exhausted. He clasped his hands on top of his head and looked far off into the distance. Wes was the only one standing – the rest were sitting, dejected, on the road, keeping away from everyone else and lost in their own thoughts.

"We're right at the beginning again... And I am so sick of this place."

Elliana sat cross-legged with her head bowed low; her hair formed a curtain and masked her face but, from the soft shaking of her shoulders, it was clear she was crying. Jack, who had sunk to the ground upon hearing Elliana's words, shifted away from her, unsure whether he should comfort her or vent his frustration at her. Lesley sat at the edge of the road, her feet on the grass and her head resting glumly on her knees.

Teddy, who had wound himself up in a fit of anger, felt the fight go out of him as he watched Elliana crumble. He now looked up at the dark blue sky and sighed miserably.

Wes paced slowly along the road, trudging through the turmoil in his mind. He looked towards the end of the road, in the direction they had been heading. It was still nothing more than a shimmer in the shadows. He turned his head and stared in the opposite direction. The road vanished into a solitary dot in the past. It was impossible to tell how far they had come or how long they had been here. All they had to track their progress was the position of the Sun, and it suggested many hours had passed.

But did that mean a couple of hours since the afternoon and now it was evening? Or had they arrived here in the morning? What would they do about food? Sleep?

So many questions, Wes contemplated. So many
questions and nobody – he glanced scornfully at
Elliana – to answer them. They were completely
alone. It was hopeless.

But, still...

Wes turned his head again to horizon ahead of them.
It was the great unknown. And it still held a certain
allure. Wes looked at the others, all of whom seemed
passed the point of caring. He wondered if they
would still go with him. Or perhaps it would be
better if he went on alone?

The others were jolted to their senses by the sound of
Wes's approaching footsteps.

"Okay," he said. "I know we're all pissed but we
need to decide what we're going to do."

Several of them stirred but nobody spoke. He went
on.

"We're in hell. And I don't know what to do about
that, but we have to keep moving."

"Why?" Jack asked, avoiding eye contact.

"Because we have to do something!" Wes snapped.

"Yes, but... What's the point?" Lesley said.

"'The point?'" Wes repeated. "The point is survival!
It's about not giving in when everything seems
hopeless! It's about facing your fears and not going
down without a fight!"

"But we've been walking for ages and found nothing," countered Jack venomously. "What's the difference between dying here and dying further along?"

"There's all the difference in the world, Jack," Wes replied.

He paused for a moment and let his words sink in. "Well, I'm going on," he continued. "I've decided I'll keep trying to find a way out. And... And maybe I should go alone."

"What? Why?" asked Teddy, rising to his feet.

"Maybe that's the mistake we've made. Maybe this is supposed to be an individual journey or whatever and we've all just got in each other's way. I think we should just do what we each feel is the right thing to do."

Teddy took a step closer to Wes and studied him closely. In a low voice that the others couldn't hear, he whispered:

"Would you really leave one of us behind?"

Wes stared coolly back at him, his tired eyes unblinking.

Jack and Lesley stood up and Teddy looked across at them. Their weariness was evident in their slow, lethargic movements.

Wes had turned away and walked slowly towards Elliana. She had not stirred and still sobbed silently. The others watched in trepidation as Wes bent down over her.

"Elliana?" he muttered in a soft, soothing voice none of them had heard him use before. "Elliana?"

She raised her head, hastily wiped her eyes and pushed her hair out of her face. She looked up at Wes in unmistakable fear.

"Elliana," he said again. "We're going to keep walking along the road."

She saw the others several metres behind Wes. They hovered hesitantly and not one of them returned her gaze.

Was this it? she thought. Was she being abandoned? She looked into Wes's inscrutable brown eyes. After what seemed like hours of tense, frozen silence, Wes held out his hand and smiled.

"Come on," he said, lifting her effortlessly to her feet. "Let's roll."

Elliana stuttered as she spoke. "Bu-but why? W-why are you helping me? I thought you... I thought you were going to leave me here."

Wes glanced at the others. "Well, yeah, the thought did cross my mind. I was angry – I still am – but I don't want to make a decision I'll regret because my head isn't in the right place. I'm not happy, and I don't know why you lied to us, but you're going to tell us everything you know now. Agreed?"

Elliana nodded silently.

"Good," said Wes. "Let's start walking."

Elliana led the way and Jack and Lesley followed. Wes waited until Teddy caught up with him.

"Of course I wouldn't leave anyone behind, Doc. Unless someone was desperate to stay. But if anyone was unsure of what to do, I still reckon we have a better chance if we stick together."

"And why's that?" asked Teddy.

Wes shrugged. "They've opened up to me and I've opened up to them. There's no judgement at all. And you know what? I feel more comfortable around them."

"So you trust everyone?"

"Oh no," replied Wes. "I don't think I trust anyone. I mean, *someone* is to blame for all of this."

Teddy was perplexed. "Then how can you be happy and content if you don't trust the people you're with?"

Again Wes shrugged. "Because they don't trust me either. We're all in this together, you know."

And with that, he turned away from Teddy and followed the others.

"You just feel better walking, don't you? You feel as if you are actually doing something productive."
"It's better than sitting doing nothing, I suppose," came the sullen reply.
They had been on the move for about five minutes and the transformation from a bare orange landscape to a rich green one was almost complete. There were many more trees surrounding them now and bushes bursting with vibrant colours but the travellers took no notice of any of it. Each of them were focused on the elusive point on the unreachable horizon.
"Okay," said Wes, who was now at the front of the group. "Elliana, do you feel alright to talk now?"
Elliana nodded and cleared her throat. "Yes, I-I think so."
"Okay," he said again. "In your own time, tell us your story."
She glanced around and saw that all eyes were fixed on her.
"I, er, I'm not really sure where to start."
"Why don't you begin by explaining why you lied to us?" Teddy blurted out.
"Teddy!" scolded Lesley.

"Leave it," warned Jack.

"That's enough!" roared Wes. "Can't you all just shut it for five minutes while the woman speaks?!"

He composed himself before continuing.

"Okay, Elliana. Why don't you just start with when you woke up here? What's the last thing you remember?"

Elliana cast her mind back. "It was night. It was dark. I don't... I was by myself, I'm sure I was heading for my friend's house. She lives just outside the town centre, it's over this long bridge and through the park."

"Did you see anyone else?" asked Lesley.

"No, it was pretty late. It's a quiet town. I guess someone could have sneaked up-- No. I'm sure I made it to the house. But then, I just can't remember."

She rubbed her eyes wearily.

"When I woke up here, the sun was quite low in the sky. It was definitely morning, so it must have been a while before you all appeared. I feared the worst at first – kidnapping, someone maybe spiked my drink, even the apocalypse – and it frightened me. I don't scare easily – I think the demons in your head are the biggest enemies you face. But this unnerved me."

She spoke with her head down. There was rapt silence every time she paused.

"I walked down the road for a while and turned over all the options in my head. As soon as I had settled on a theory, I saw Teddy and Lesley in the distance."

"What was your theory?" asked Teddy.

"You'll find out once I've told you who I am," she replied.

Before Teddy could respond, Lesley cut in.

"I *knew* someone was following us! Why didn't you say anything?"

Elliana shrugged and smiled guiltily.

"I thought it was funny," she whispered. "And--" she continued over their indignant protests. "I still wasn't sure what was going on. What if you two had been the ones that had kidnapped me?"

"But if you followed them," said Jack. "And you heard what they were saying. *And* after they met us and it was obvious none of us were a threat – why didn't you say something then?!"

She smiled her guilty smile again. "Well, I'd done it that long, and I thought it was quite funny so I just decided to... keep it up."

Everyone stared at her, dumbstruck.

"You thought it was '*quite funny*'?" repeated Teddy angrily.

"We were terrified!" exclaimed Lesley.

"So was I," Elliana responded. "And after I realised you weren't a threat I thought about revealing myself so many times but every time I thought about it I just found the whole thing laughable. It's like you said earlier, Teddy - this whole place, this situation, it's just ludicrous. And it made me laugh. I know I waited too long for any of you to find it funny but I just couldn't help myself."

"That's not funny," said Wes.

"You're insane," seethed Teddy.

Elliana stared coolly at them both. "Surely you know people respond differently to a crisis. Well this was my way: to accept I was in a bad situation and to make the most of it."

"'*Making the most of it*'!" cried Teddy. "This is real life! You can't just make the most out of *this* situation!"

"Why not?" said Elliana.

"Because this is REAL LIFE!" repeated Teddy.

"Says who? Everyone seems pretty convinced we're all dreaming right now so why are you so worried about playing by the rules? Why is it *your* problem if I choose to act a certain way?"

"Then why are you acting like this? Why are you acting like it's all a joke? What made you this way?"

Elliana smiled widely and stifled a giggle.

In a matter of minutes she had regained much of her composure and control.

She raised her head and looked towards Teddy.

"I grew up. And that was a terrible mistake. I was miserable for ages. And nothing changed until I met Louise."

"Who's Louise?" asked Jack.

"She's my friend from university. Well, sort of. And she came along right when I needed her."

"What do you mean?" said Teddy. Curiosity had softened his tone.

"When I hit my twenties, I started to feel a bit down. Not full-on depression, nothing too serious. I just felt sad. A lot. I would forget about it when I was doing things, like if I was with friends or studying, or reading, you know. But when it was just me and my thoughts, I always came back to this sort of default setting where I always felt really down. Eventually it snowballed and, as I got to the end of uni, I barely did anything. I fell into a routine where I would study and watch TV every day. And I was totally unprepared for life after uni. It was big and scary and unknown and I just couldn't contemplate it so I put it to the back of my mind. But, of course, you can't hide from your problems forever and it all started eating away at me. So something had to change."

She took a deep breath and slowly released it.

"You just decided to change your life there and then on your own?" asked Teddy, sounding impressed.

Elliana looked sideways at him. "I guess you don't come across many people with that sort of strength in your line of work?"

"Not really, no," he admitted sheepishly. "Of course, if everyone had that strength, drive, courage, and creativity then I would be out of a job..."

Elliana smiled. "I wish I had been a strong enough person to do that. But I wasn't back then. I needed someone to guide me. I guess we all do at that age." She glanced at Jack who smiled warmly at her.

"So how did you find your guide?" he asked.

"Totally by accident," laughed Elliana. "Or maybe it was destiny? I haven't decided yet."

"Even now," said Wes wearily, "you can't give us a straight answer?"

"Alright, sorry, sorry," she said. "Anyway, the first time I met her was just before I finished uni. She had come to visit one of her friends who happened to be my flatmate. We were about the same age – give or take a year or two – and I was fascinated by her. While all of my flatmates were worrying about internships, careers, interviews, and prospects, this girl turns up like a hurricane, blowing away all the cobwebs and telling us to focus on being happy. We'd all been cooped up for a long time as the climax of our education neared so the flat was a tense place to be. Everyone was walking on eggshells. But Louise turned up, out of the blue, and brought this amazing energy and colour to our lives.

"I remember setting my books down and leaving my room for the first time in days and found her on the couch in the living room. She was laughing hysterically. You have to understand how fractious the flat was back then, so this foreign laughter just smashed through it all. We would chat for hours. Sometimes she would just let me go on and on while she listened and occasionally commented.

"After that first night, I felt lighter than I had done in months. I had voiced a lot of my concerns and worries and suddenly I didn't feel so down. But it was more than that. Louise told me about everything she had done in the three or four years since she had left school and I listened in amazement. No college, no uni, no fretting over job applications. She had packed a bag and went in search of happiness. The stories she told, the things she had done, the people she had met – she painted this vibrant picture of a world I never even knew existed. I didn't just feel happier; I felt free.

"For the first time in my life, I felt it was actually *my* life. Like I could go wherever I wanted because it was *my* journey. I could walk away from my degree because it would be *my* choice. I could make mistakes because they would be *my* mistakes..."

She gazed, misty-eyed, into the distance.

They walked on for nearly a minute, allowing Elliana to lose herself in her own memories, before Wes could take it no longer.

"So you quit your degree? A girl comes along with a nice smile and you throw away your education?"

Elliana snapped back to the present. "Of course not. I couldn't find any justification for dropping out of uni, especially not at that point. But it meant I was more relaxed going into the exams and I didn't fear the future anymore. The main lesson I took away from university was the fact that I didn't very much like university."

Lesley snorted and Elliana stared at her.

"Oh no," said Lesley quickly. "I felt the same way! I just think you summed it up very succinctly."

Elliana laughed.

"Yes, well, I don't regret going altogether because I enjoyed it at the time and I suppose that's the most important thing. I just wish I'd done more of the things I wanted to do when I left school, instead of doing what I felt I *should* have done.

"Louise and I would talk all day and night about our lives and our dreams, our hopes and our regrets. After a day in her company, I felt like I had woken up after having been asleep for so long. It was like looking back on a half-remembered dream. She really made you smile, you know. She made you feel hopeful for the future."

She trailed off again and the others waited patiently.

Further on they walked, each person casting their eyes towards the horizon with Elliana's words ringing in their ears. A swirl of leaves scattered across the road by their feet and the grass whispered playfully on either side.

"Louise stayed for a week or two but it was all over in the blink of an eye. As suddenly as she had arrived she then disappeared. Off on another adventure somewhere new."

"What, just like that she was gone?" asked Jack. Elliana nodded glumly.

"I think it's always the same with these kinds of people," began Teddy. "The wild ones, the explorers, the ones who irrevocably change us – they breeze into our life with such colour and beauty and then leave it so abruptly, like a shooting star across the sky."

"Yes, that sounds like her," smiled Elliana.

"Where did she go?" Lesley asked. "Somewhere exotic?"

"I'm not sure," Elliana replied. "Possibly. Although it was never about the countries or the travelling for her. It was about the people she met along the way. And I'm pleased I get to count myself as one of those people."

Jack smiled. "That's a lovely way of putting it."

Elliana nodded again. "She left me a present of sorts. Her diary. Or part of it at least. She had torn a couple of pages out and left them for me."

"What was on the pages?" murmured Wes.

"Her entries for the week she stayed with us. And a letter she had written for me. I knew she kept a diary but I thought it was just for the interesting things that happened in her life. I never imagined she'd bother writing about us."

"What did she say? Can you remember?"

"Of course," Elliana smiled. "I memorised every word. The letter was really nice because it spoke directly to me; she said I should go out into the world and find the people and the experiences that would make me really happy. But the diary entry was more special, I think. Probably because she had written it for herself – it was like she had left some of her thoughts with me. There it was, sitting on my bed, just an explosion of colours and patterns. I picked it up and started reading..."

'I came to visit Michelle for a day or two. I've not seen her since before Christmas but we're never at home at the same time so I decided I'll take the chance while I'm nearby. She's pretty stressed with the exams looming so I didn't want to bug her too much. I can't believe she'll be a doctor in a few years!

Anyway, I was chatting to her flatmates and that's when I met Elliana. She's incredible. She was stressed as well but you wouldn't know it when you spoke to her. She's so kind and generous and I listened to her talk for ages. I don't know why she's studying geology because it's clearly not her passion. She always talks about wanting to help people and I think she'd be AMAZING at it.

It's her sense of humour and her outlook on life. She's so wonderfully weird. Elliana has a gift and I wish she would share it with the world. She was so much fun and had this amazing energy that I decided to stay for over a week! But I don't mind because meeting her really made me think a lot about how people see the world and how maybe I could change for the better? She makes me want to be a better person and I can't really give her a higher compliment than that.

I hope she travels a bit and sees more of the world and spreads her happiness wherever she goes. It breaks my heart to think of a spark like hers being extinguished. She has everything she needs to make a difference in the world. All she needs is a shove out the door!!!'

"I don't know, maybe it sounds silly," Elliana continued. "But it meant a lot to me. It's the kind of advice everyone needs at one stage or another. For me, it was extraordinary that this kind of wisdom was coming from someone so young. And someone I really respected, too."

There was another period of silence while they pondered her words.

"That's so nice," said Lesley at last.

"It made me smile," said Elliana. "The fact that someone had taken the time to write that for me. I wasn't expecting it. I was just enjoying the time spent with a friend."

"That's what friendship is," said Teddy. "To share those moments and have that bond with another person. I think you're lucky to have met someone who was willing to give you a beautiful representation of that connection."

Elliana smiled again and her bottom lip quivered. Her eyes filled with tears.

"Yes, that's her. That's Louise."

"What I don't understand," began Jack. "If she wrote that in her own diary then why did she leave it for you?"

"I'm not sure, although I would guess that it's because Louise decided I needed it a lot more than she did."

"So then what happened?" Wes blurted out.
Elliana was taken aback by his bluntness.
"Sorry," said Wes. "I just don't see how we get from you getting your friend's diary to you deciding it's funny to stalk us in the desert."
"Okay, you're right, sorry. I'll fast forward."
"Just tell us what you did after that and leading up to this place," Wes said hurriedly, then he smiled to show he was still interested.
"What you have to understand is how happy I was. I wasn't singing and dancing in the throes of ecstasy all day – it wasn't like that. It was a feeling of contentment. I was happy in what I was doing. So the flat became a nicer place to live because we were laughing and joking a lot more."
"But the real change was within you?" prompted Teddy.
"Definitely. I found it easier to laugh so I suppose I really got my sense of humour back. I'd be loud and silly and I'd... I don't know, I just tried to find the humour in every situation. And when I was with people as well, it was so much easier. I always found it very easy to get along with others; sometimes it was their reactions and sometimes it was when they joined in the fun I was having. Those moments still make me smile."
Teddy rolled his eyes and sighed heavily.

"So *that's* why you followed us and kept it a secret?"
"Yes, sorry," she replied guiltily. "I didn't mean to at first – I was wary of you all – but then I had the idea to stealthily follow you..."
"But why did you pretend you were some kind of expert here?" asked Lesley. "And those answers you were giving – what was all that about?"
"By that point, I was pretty sure I knew what this place was – some kind of dream that we're all part of, and the only way out is by recognising what changes you need to make in your life. You know, something simple and boring but it would make a good story. So, when I started speaking to you, I decided to give you lots of melodramatic clues pointing you in that direction. Oh, and also because it was winding Wes up."
Wes scoffed.
"But what did you do after Louise left?" asked Jack pointedly.
Elliana, who was still smiling mischievously at Wes, switched her attention to Jack.
"Yes, sorry, I keep getting sidetracked," she said.
"Well, I finished university then I thought about all the plans I was going to make. I had a list of countries, I researched travel jobs, I started a blog... I planned for ages. That was probably my first mistake."

"The planning?"

"Yes. Because I was so excited planning my adventure that I didn't go out and actually live it. It was too easy to convince myself I was already doing something worthwhile. And I always had excuses for not starting out."

"Excuses?"

"The main one was money. I convinced myself I didn't have enough money to travel and I should get a short-term job, save up, and be thorough about my route."

"Well, that's understandable. When was that?"

"Two years ago."

"Two--? What? You've been on the cusp of leaving to go travel for two years and yet you're still in the same job?"

"Yeah," Elliana said miserably. "Two years. I was supposed to go and save the world and I haven't done a thing."

"Do you hate your job?"

Elliana thought for moment. "No, actually. Obviously it's not what I wish I was doing but it's alright. And the people are so nice and funny. We always make the days fun."

"So... Apart from the fact you clearly want to go and travel, do you regret working there?"

She didn't answer although she was clearly thinking deeply.

"It's just that..." Jack went on. "I would think that if you feel you learned anything from your friend, Louise, it would be to have fun and be happy. And make others around you happy. I mean, isn't that what you've been doing?"

"He's right," agreed Lesley.

"From what I've heard," Teddy started. "Your passion lies in making other people happy, releasing them from tension and making the days more enjoyable. It seems to me that your friend simply wanted you to be aware of this. And perhaps she wanted as many people as possible to be in your presence. To witness your gift. It's a wonderful thing to bring happiness and laughter into the world."

"But the travelling..." Elliana muttered, her voice breaking.

"To hell with the travelling!" replied Teddy. "It's overrated. If it's people you need, you'll find them wherever you go. You don't need to see the Taj Mahal to know it's there. Or walk the Champs Elysée to know it is iconic. You're not the kind of person to achieve happiness by looking at landmarks. Besides, you have the internet for that!

"If you really want to see the world, you will. And the fun you'll have! But it won't fulfil you in the same way. Because it means more to you to bring a smile to a sad face. And if that is what you have been doing then it has not been wasted time."

He looked steadily at Elliana.

"Don't waste time living someone else's life."

The silence that followed was the longest yet. Elliana's eyes slowly welled up again and she looked up beyond the trees. Vast swathes of the deepest blue swept across the sky, slowly morphing into purple in the very corners of the canvas. The slight breeze had returned, sending leaves dancing above their heads in a swirl of colour.

"You know, it really is beautiful here," said Jack at last, his words rising into the sky.

Chapter Ten

It was a long time before anyone spoke. Even Wes, who had seemed anxious to hear Elliana's story, kept quiet while the five of them continued along the road. Memories and questions wove in and out of their minds like waves crashing upon a beach, overlapping and disappearing all at once.

Teddy let out a long, low whistle. "I'm curious," he said. "Why were you so sure this is all a dream?"

Elliana thought for a moment, then said, plainly: "Because what else can it be?"

"Well, this could all be real, for starters," said Lesley. "We could actually be in some foreign country, away from civilisation."

"Do you really believe that?" asked Elliana sceptically.

Lesley did not answer.

"I don't know," said Elliana. "The human mind is tricky, it can make us see things that aren't there and, I know it's a stretch, but maybe it could create a dream as vivid as this."

"So why are we all dreaming the same thing?" asked Jack.

"We could all simply be projections of each other's subconscious," mooted Teddy. "But I'm starting to seriously doubt that."

"Why?"

"Because it's so detailed. There's four other people sharing this dream with each of us and we've learned so much about each other's past. I think that dreams gloss over a lot of the detail but this '*experience*' has been meticulous."

Wes started. "So where does that leave us? You *don't* think we're dreaming?"

Teddy pulled a pained expression.

"I..." he hesitated. "I don't think this is some virtual event and, despite how real this physically feels, I can't see us being awake somewhere. It would suggest we've been kidnapped or journeyed here ourselves and, to me, the idea that that's all happened is just not plausible."

The group mulled over his words for a while.

"You mentioned your theory," Wes muttered, turning to Elliana, "about why you were here. What was it again?"

"Oh," she said. "It's, well, it sounds a bit silly now."

"Silly is better than nothing," said Jack wisely.

Elliana exhaled deeply.

"Alright," she said. "I assumed that I had been brought here (or put in a dream state or fallen asleep) for some reason. Obviously, there must be a reason behind it. Someone wants me to learn something. And I decided that the only way for me to 'escape' was to figure out the change I needed to make in my own life. Maybe there were some regrets or some problem I had to solve, I don't know. I'm sorry, that probably sounds really stupid."

"It's as good as anything we've got," said Wes. "What did you decide you had to change?"

"I thought," she said sheepishly, "that it was about me putting off my 'dream' of travelling. Like this was a wake-up call telling to live my life or seize the day. But after talking to all of you..."

"You realised you were in the right place all along?" prompted Jack.

Elliana nodded. "Maybe that was the 'truth' I was looking for. Maybe it's what I needed to hear."

She ran a hand through her hair.

"There is one other thing I, sort of, decided on," she said. "It's just a thought but I felt it confirmed something I was unsure of."

"What's that?"

"Well, I assumed someone brought me here because I needed to learn some lesson, right?"

The others nodded.

"And I can only think of one person who would care that I learn that lesson. In this manner."

"Who?"

Elliana shrugged. "Me."

Wes looked sceptical.

"Think about it," Elliana continued. "It would confirm that this is all a dream. I mean, if it was real, then I would remember bringing myself here, wouldn't I? And, besides, who else would go to all that bother?"

Wes looked at the others. They were thinking carefully. Jack nodded slightly.

"I think it makes sense," he said. "I mean, what else have we got?"

"Okay, let me get this straight," Wes uttered. "We all brought ourselves here. We're probably all dreaming. And the reason we are here is to solve some problems in our life?"

Teddy smiled and gave a non-committal jerk of his head.

"Basically."

"So," Wes stopped walking and the others turned to look at him. "What is this, some kind of group therapy?"

Teddy laughed.

"If that's true – bearing in mind we've been here for hours – then whoever set this up is going to make a fortune on our bill."

They all chuckled then resumed walking. Everything felt a little clearer in their minds now they had spoken at length. Thoughts turned to whatever each person considered their own shortcomings and how they had opened up about their lives.

Communicating with the others had certainly helped ease their burdens. However...

Lesley furrowed her brow. "There's just one thing I don't understand."

"What is it?" asked Elliana.

"If we've all shared our problems, talked it through at length, and learned our lessons, then why haven't we woke up back home? Why isn't the dream over for us?"

Teddy shifted uncomfortably. Catching sight of this, Elliana murmured: "I would imagine it's because not all of us have shared our story."

All eyes landed on Teddy. His smile had disappeared and he looked vulnerable.

"What? Me?" he stuttered.

"She's right," said Wes.

"We've all shared *our* stories," said Jack.

"But I don't have a story," Teddy retorted. "I don't have any problems!"

"Why?" asked Wes. "Because you deal with people with problems all the time and you think you're better than them?"

"No!" Teddy replied angrily. "Never!"

"Do you think you're better than us?"

"Of course not!"

"Wes..." warned Lesley.

"I'm just saying," defended Wes, "that there must be a reason he's not telling us his story."

"There probably is a reason," Elliana spoke. "But we can't force him to open up."

"If we're stuck here because of him--"

"It's none of our business--"

"You can't force him to--"

"*I want to know why he won't--*"

"BECAUSE IT HURTS!" yelled Teddy and silence fell immediately.

There were pools of tears in his eyes.

He exhaled and wiped his eyes roughly with his hands.

"Because it hurts," he repeated in a broken voice.

He turned away from them and walked off the road. At the foot of a nearby tree he bowed his head and lowered himself to the ground. The others watched solemnly as he sat himself dully against the trunk with his knees pulled up to his chest. He looked defeated.

Wes moved towards him slowly and sat on the edge of the road. They faced each other and Wes hesitated. He tried to communicate his contrition wordlessly. Teddy nodded sadly.

In time, Elliana, Lesley, and Jack sat, too, each one of them facing the psychiatrist.

"Please, Teddy," Lesley murmured. "Please tell us what's wrong. I can't bear to see you in pain."

Teddy waited a long time before replying. He composed himself and let out a deep sigh.

"It's a long story," he whispered.

Elliana smiled warmly. "Aren't they all...?"

*

Bracing himself against the biting, horizontal wind, Teddy pulled his scarf tighter and stuffed his hands deep into his pockets. The blare of noise from the busy street was drowned out by the howling cacophony emanating from the elements. The rain, which had pelted the pavements before Teddy left his office, exhausted itself as he rounded the corner onto his street. He continued at a brisk pace, stumbling as he remembered, too late, to negotiate the large puddle which accumulated over the crevice between the kerb and the road. Cursing his absent-mindedness, he shook his foot and thick water drops flew in every direction.

At that moment, he felt his phone vibrating in his pocket.

"Hello?!" he called irritably over the noise.

There was little or no reply. All he could distinguish was a faint whisper, although that may have been the whistling wind across the earpiece.

"Hello!" he called out again.

"Teddy?" came Sarah's voice on the other end.

Probably phoning to chastise me for being late, Teddy thought.

"Yes? I've had a hell of day, Sarah!"

"Teddy, where are you?"

He did not notice her toneless delivery.

"I'm... I'm at home, Teddy. I think we... Look, where are you?"

"I'm on my way!" Teddy replied shrilly. "Can't you hear the wind? I'm obviously walking back now."

There was a pause before Sarah responded.

"Right, okay, I... I suppose I'll wai--"

"You wouldn't believe it, today!" Teddy cut across her. "Three sessions ran over, meaning I had three late appointments (and obviously that's all *my* fault, isn't it?) and totally missed lunch and then--"

He broke off while he yelled at a cyclist who had nearly collided with him.

"Sorry, goddamn cyclists... Anyway, a family member of one of my patients barged into my office today! Can you believe it? A *family member!* Screaming bloody murder at me that I was to blame for this and that..."

"Listen, Teddy," Sarah started as he trailed off. "Just get back as soon as possible, okay? I need--"

"Well, of course, I've just told you I'm coming back, didn't I?"

"Yes," Sarah replied quietly. "Okay, I'll see you, 'bye."

With that, she hung up. Teddy stared at his phone. Now, that's one temperamental woman! he thought. If she wasn't my fiancé, she'd be an interesting patient herself!

He thrust the phone back into his pocket and moaned at the weather. Fighting against the wind, he paced quickly, his front steps visible about fifty feet ahead. Sarah had been a wonderful woman, Teddy reminisced. When they had first met, she was the brightest girl in the class, full of charm and wit. They had so much fun when they were younger, especially those university days. No period since had ever reached those happy heights of youthful exuberance. They shared their views on the world and their dreams for the future. Teddy had his five- and ten-year plans worked out whereas Sarah was more relaxed when it came to schedules and projections for what lay ahead. Teddy had always felt that this was the reason they worked together as a couple. Once Sarah decided on a solid career, however, they would be completely happy.

When he reached the steps, Teddy took them two at a time and swiftly extricated his key from his coat, eager to shelter from the cold. Upon swinging the door shut behind him, he let out a happy moan of comfort as he bathed in the warmth of the hall. It was then that he saw Sarah.

She stood stoically, perfectly upright with her hands hanging limply by her sides. Her eyes were wide and unreadable and her lips pursed closely together. Standing obediently next to her were two large suitcases, both of which were clearly full.

Teddy watched her, dumbstruck. Something was wrong but his brain could not process it. All he felt was a sickening pain that seemed to hollow out his gut. Gradually, as he pieced together the picture, he felt the dread spread through every inch of his body. His mouth relaxed and he tried to speak.

"S-Sarah?" he murmured incoherently.

Sarah's eyes filled with tears but her facial expression did not change. She maintained her steely, resolute stance. With a great force of will, she cleared her throat and spoke.

"Teddy, this... This isn't easy. It's..." she paused to compose herself and continued through the tears.

"This is the hardest thing I've ever had to do."

"B-but why?" Teddy said at last, his voice cracking.

"We've been falling apart," she said. "For a long time. We've both felt it, we both know it hasn't been working."

"Wha-- When?"

"We've been resenting each other for months, years even. Happy in our little comfort zone but it's been eating away at both of us. We're totally different people to who we were back... back then, when we first met."

Teddy took a step towards her and stopped. He looked around himself as if searching for proof that it was really happening. He put his hands to his temples and attempted to process the truth of what he was hearing.

"I don't think it's been that bad," he said quietly and in a voice he did not recognise. "I mean, we've had some tough days... an-- and we've both been stressed a lot recently... It's not been that bad..."

"It has Teddy. It really has. Look at us – we've been spending more time at work and less time with each other--"

"Exactly," Teddy cut in. "We should take more time to be with each other."

"No," Sarah said sadly. "Us, our relationship... it's the reason we're spending more time at work, away from each other and away from the friction."

Teddy felt his eyes stinging. This couldn't be happening. It was all wrong.

"I..." Sarah began. She paused and locked eyes with her fiancé. "I am so unhappy every day, Teddy. And it's not your fault. It's because we don't belong together. I can feel myself becoming a worse person. And I see it happening to you, too. You are so kind-hearted and generous, my love, and you help so many people. But this... this *strife*, this *discord* between us is slowly eating away all that love and happiness. And I don't want us to resent each other." Teddy thought, slowly, mechanically. He could not stop staring at the ring on Sarah's finger.

"I love you, Edward, as a person and as a friend. So much. And I know you love me too. But we will tear each other apart if we stay together like this. Please, you must understand this."

"I don't agree..." he mumbled.

"It doesn't mean I love you any less. I care for you more than anyone else in the world. I just love you in a different way."

"Of course that means you love me less," Teddy protested. "You're choosing not to be with me! Something has changed."

"I don't bring out the best in you anymore. I don't make you a better person. I don't even make you want to *be* a better person... We're not the same people we were."

Teddy coughed into his fist and fidgeted with his hands. He took another step forward until they were close enough to touch.

"Well, wh-what if we make an effort to be more like our younger selves? We'll go back to those days!"

It was his last, desperate hope.

Sarah placed her hand softly on Teddy's cheek. He twitched slightly at the contact but fixed his eyes on hers. She shook her head sadly.

"We are who we are," she whispered. "We can't change that. And we can't relive the past."

They stood in the same position for a long time, feeling the romantic bonds holding them together gradually unravel. It was a moment too tender for words.

Eventually, although it went against everything he felt able to do, although it broke his heart a thousand times over, Teddy smiled.

"What a past we've had together," he said.

And then the tears engulfed them. Closely they held each other, closer than they had felt in years, with comfort and understanding communicated silently between them.

Pain would come, eventually, and for both of them, but for now they held on, letting the peaceful goodbye run its course.

Chapter Eleven

"It's strange, isn't it?" Teddy spoke into the reverent silence that followed his tale. "You never really consider that psychiatrists need therapy. You forget that they feel the same pain that can crush the lives of other people."

He looked at the understanding faces.

"Not that we're better people," he added. "That's not what I mean. It's just not a thought that usually springs up in the mind."

He exhaled and looked up to the sky. Almost all the blue had faded into purple. The sun kissed the rippling horizon.

"When did it happen?" asked Wes quietly. He averted his eyes and did not expect a reply.

Teddy blinked several times, his head still inclined upwards.

"Three months ago," he muttered.

Eyes widened in shock.

"Three months?!" repeated Lesley.

Teddy lowered his gaze to her. "Relatively speaking," he smiled.

"And how... how have you been since then?"

"Oh, I've been better," he replied dryly.

"You must've been together for years if--"

"Seven years."

"Wow," said Jack. "Listen, Teddy, I really don't know what to say..."

"It's okay, Jack."

"I can't even imagine... I mean, that length of time... How would you handle something like that?"

"As best I can. By working, by really trying to help people."

"I'm really sorry, Teddy," said Lesley. "I feel terrible because you've spoken with us about all of our issues. You've helped us all and I... I just don't know if I'll be able to return the favour."

"It's okay, I'll recover in time. You don't have to help me."

"Sure we do," Wes exclaimed. "You were there for us. We trusted you with our past and you helped us look forward to the future."

"I'm sorry, Wes, but this isn't a problem you can solve."

"True. We might not be able to cure you or fix everything. But we can listen. We can help you by giving you our time. It's the absolute least we owe you."

The others murmured in agreement.

"You could start by telling us how you feel," said Elliana.

"I'm fine."

"You're clearly not. Come on, tell us... Tell us what happened next in your story."

Teddy looked from face to face. They were all attentive, a mix of curiosity and care. He took a deep breath.

"Sarah moved out, she went to live with a friend of hers and then moved overseas. And I stayed in the house. It was half a house really. All of her stuff was gone and the place felt eerie and lonely. I missed her so much the first couple of weeks. I... I, er," he cleared his throat, "I cried a lot at first. I even had to sleep in a different room because... because the bedroom still smelled like her...

"I took a short leave of absence from work and went back home to sort myself out. I met my old friends, my family, and I tried to adjust to my life as an 'I' not as a 'We'."

He breathed deeply again.

"How did that go?"

"Tough. It was a really tough time for me. Occasionally it became a little overwhelming, but I came back to my house a few weeks later feeling better than I had done in a long time. It was nice taking a break from my own life and immersing myself in someone else's. My friends and I would reminisce about younger days, before life became so serious. And I guess that's what I realised – that I took it too seriously. I planned my career out from the moment I left school. And I lived for the future instead of living in the present."

Jack nodded. "I know it's not the same... But when I visited Marcus after all that time, the years just melted away and we spoke about the fun we used to have, the trouble we would get into, the friends we would make. Afterwards, I felt lighter, freer. It was as if I was looking at myself as a grown up and wondering what the hell had happened to me! I'd forgotten what it was like to have fun."

Teddy smiled. "Yes, it was something like that. In a way it was like going back in time...

"Once I got back to my house, I thought long and hard about what I wanted. I remember... I remember wishing the younger Sarah was there to talk to. We used to know each other inside out and, whenever I had a problem, she would know the answer. Or she would point me in the right direction. But my Sarah was long gone. And it was only me now."

"What did you do?"

"Well, I eventually realised that I had to go back to work. Regardless of all the turmoil in my life, I still love what I do. And, for the time being, I will give myself over fully to helping anyone I could."

"And did that help?"

"Yes and no. It helped distract me. And I did focus on my work a lot – I was able to completely focus on the other person. But, outside office hours, I was a mess. I lost sight of the person I was and defined myself totally by my work. It was like starting all over again... How do you pick up the pieces of a broken life?"

Teddy stared blankly at his hands.

"We're no longer talking in the past tense, are we?" said Lesley.

Wes caught on. "You're still recovering," he remarked to Teddy.

"Life is not always easy," said Elliana. "But I don't believe we are ever given more than we can handle."

Wes cleared his throat. "I don't know much, and I obviously haven't been through what you have, but maybe you just need a little time? The worst part of my life was when my dad went. It devastated me at the time. And for months I didn't feel anything. But eventually I healed. Do I still get upset thinking about him? Of course I do. But maybe that's not a bad thing... because I'm reminded of all the good things as well..."

Lesley put her hand on his arm. "I was a lot younger than you when I suffered so I don't know if it compares, but I still get pangs of sadness. Having said that, I would say I healed eventually. It just took time and the love of some close friends."

Jack fidgeted with his hands, absent-mindedly pulling blades of grass from the ground.

"Do..." he hesitated. "Have you managed to forgive Sarah?"

Teddy looked at him squarely but it was Elliana who spoke first.

"Forgive her? For what? She's done nothing wrong as far as I can tell."

Jack's eyes widened in surprise and his gaze flicked quickly between Elliana and Teddy. Teddy, however did not explode in anger. He merely stared at Elliana as if waiting for her to expand.

"Well, first of all, you both shared many happy times together, didn't you? From what I've heard, you spent your early twenties in the company of someone who thought you were wonderful and made you a better person. That sort of happiness, that contentment - that's what everyone needs at that age! I got to spend a week with someone who made me feel special – you got half a decade."

Teddy reacted slowly. He opened his mouth to respond but Elliana continued.

"You may have stretched the relationship passed its breaking point but she was open and honest with you when she decided to end it. I know it's not ideal calling off an engagement but isn't it better she spoke up before you were married? Before you had kids? Instead of forcing you to live a lie, she set you free."

The others stared in amazement. Teddy's facial expression had not changed.

"I'm just telling you what my opinion is, Teddy. Believe me – I'm not taking sides. But can I ask you a question?"

He nodded slightly.

"Are you angry at Sarah for ending it? Or are you just upset that it's over?"

She left the question hanging in the air. Nobody else moved a muscle.

Finally, Teddy started. His cheeks twitched and, incredibly, turned into a smile.

"You know," he said in a rough voice. "I was never angry at her. I had no right to be. And yes, I'm upset that it's over but it's..." he rubbed his face while searching for the words. "I'm not even angry... I was in shock for a long time and my body is still dealing with it. I feel I've dealt with it emotionally but I'm not over it yet. I don't understand why, on the whole, I've been so calm. It's... it's like..."

"Like you know she was right all along? That you were never meant to be?"

Elliana looked searchingly at Teddy. He looked tired but it was something more than mere physical exertion. He was exhausted. And it made him seem a lot older than he was.

"You're right," he said quietly. "Maybe I always knew it but fooled myself. Maybe I convinced myself that the love Sarah and I shared was something more. Or something else."

He stood up and dusted himself down, wiping away a solitary tear as he did so. Lesley rose, too, and moved closer to him.

"You have a kind heart, Teddy. "And I feel blessed to know you."

"Thank you," he murmured.

One by one they stepped back on to the road.

Beneath the darkening purple sky, everyone stood facing each other.

"We have a decision to make here," said Wes. "And we need to sort some things out."

"Like what?" asked Jack.

"Well, there's the major issue first of all. We don't know who to trust. We have to consider the possibility that one of us is to blame for all of this." He looked around at all of them.

"I'm saying this, not to cause friction, but because the time has come for the truth."

Eyes darted from one person to another.

"If anyone knows *anything* about what's going on, *now* is the time to speak."

Nobody moved.

"I don't know what's going on," said Jack, putting his hands up. "I don't know where we are and, frankly, that scares me a little bit. However, if I found out that someone here set this all up then... then it would upset me more than I can say... and I don't know what I might do to that person."

Others murmured in agreement.

"Okay, looks like no one has anything to admit to," said Wes. "In that case, there's something I would like to say."

Everyone watched him warily as he stood, hands on his hips, surveying each of them.

"We've shared stories from our lives with each other. I've spoken about things I've never spoken to anyone else about, and I'm sure I'm not the only one that can say that today."

He paused and took a deep breath.

"I have trusted all of you with my past. And now I'm going to trust you with my future too."

After another long pause, Teddy nodded.

"I'm frustrated, I'm unhappy, I'm lost," he said. "But I trust everyone here and that's no little thing."

"Me too," echoed Elliana and Lesley.

"Hear hear," cheered Jack.

"Good, that's sorted then," said Wes. "The other thing, and I know we've talked these theories to death, but have we all agreed where we *think* we are?"

"Dream?" answered Lesley.

"Dream," nodded Elliana confidently.

The others agreed.

"And, finally," Wes went on. "There's something else we need to decide."

"What's that?" Jack asked.

Wes looked up to the sky. The velvet sky had darkened further and half the Sun had disappeared.

"It will be dark soon. Too dark to see where we're going, I would imagine, unless there's three moons here at night. So we need to decide whether we should keep walking or stop here for the night."

"What? Camp out here?"

Wes nodded. "There's enough trees and bushes to shelter us from the wind – it's been pretty unpredictable today. And I'm not sure about the temperature. It's been warm enough through the day, even recently as the Sun's gone down it's been pretty mild."

"What about a fire?" asked Jack. "Could we build one?"

They looked around. There was plenty of wood nearby.

"Possibly. I'll do what I can," Wes said.

Lesley turned and looked towards the dim horizon. Before long, it would disappear from view.

"I don't really like the idea of stopping, but I think it's probably the most sensible thing to do. *If* Wes can make a fire, of course!"

Elliana pondered for moment. "If we are supposed to find something along the road, we would probably miss it in the dark anyway. Let's wait until daylight."

"Agreed," echoed Jack and Teddy.

"Okay, great," said Wes. "We'll try and collect wood and dried leaves for the next five or ten minutes while we still have the light. I'll see what I can do with the fire."

"Do we need anything else?" asked Lesley.

"Some blankets and a hot chocolate would be fantastic!" called Jack as he went in search of wood.

Some time later, the Sun slipped fully beyond the horizon and faint stars began to litter the sky. The beautiful purple mosaic had morphed into a still black, with gentle wisps of white cloud illuminated by starlight.

The only other light in the lonely world was one of a crackling orange and red: Wes's fire burned gently at the side of the road, showering flickers of heat and light all around.

"I was wondering," Elliana spoke into the night. "If we are sharing this dream, then what's to stop others coming along, too?"

Jack looked nervously over his shoulder.

"No, I don't mean right now, or in the middle of the night. But, what if this happens to other people? What if more people come here in the future?"

"What if more people have been here in the past?" mooted Teddy.

"Exactly. Maybe we won't all dream of the same wasteland so they might appear elsewhere, but what if they did come here? What if someone came along who knew where we actually were?"

"That would be nice," said Jack. "I miss home."

Wes placed another piece of wood on the fire.

"Do you think you will do anything differently," he asked quietly, "when you get home?"

Jack thought for a long time. He cast his mind back, retracing his own journey that day. He thought of football, the game – and career – he loved so much. He thought of his manager and the kindness and understanding he had shown him; and he thought of Marcus, whom he owed so much to for his friendship.

"In all honesty, no, I don't think I would change a lot of things. It was nice realising that the things I should be doing are the things I already *have* been doing, if that makes sense? I feel like the main thing I learned today was to be thankful for the things, and people, I have. And maybe now that I know more about myself, I can use that to help others. I could give something back to the people and the communities that I owe so much to."

"Wow, Jack, that's... that's lovely," said Lesley. "And I think it's very inspiring to hear you talk with such passion."

Jack smiled bashfully. "What about you, Lesley? What will you change?"

Lesley considered. She felt empowered and eager. Eager to make a change in her own life. All she had needed was someone to point it out for her. She thought about the others and how they had opened their lives to each other and trusted in the compassion of everyone else. That was really amazing. It required the innocence of a child, something she knew all about.

"I'd love to help others in the way that people have helped me. You've all said some really beautiful things to me today and I'll never forget them. I feel like it's given me the inspiration I needed to start something up. I don't think I'll march into my work and quit in a blaze of glory or anything like that. But the second I get back, if I get back, I'm going to contact charities and volunteer organisations. I'm not going to sit about and wait for my life to begin because that is time that some children just don't have. And... And I'm going to do it. I'm going to start my own orphanage, if I can. Or help expand one. Whatever. I'm going to save as many people as I can."

She looked above the fire and saw everyone smiling warmly at her.

"That's really fantastic, Lesley. I know you'll be a success," said Elliana.

"You're such a great person," Wes said. "I hope you do it, I hope you go out and save the world."

"Thank you," she replied. "And I really hope you find what you're looking for, Wes, whatever that is."

Wes smiled and thought about his life back home. He had definitely lost some direction when his father died. He did not dislike the army. It was a job. It was enjoyable. But when he thought of those days growing up, it was his friends, his family and the community he remembered. The days of impromptu football matches, everyone huddled around his father, hanging on his every word. A large of group of people who just happened to live near one another, enjoying each other's company as if they were lifelong friends.

"I think I'd like to emulate my dad. Not copy him, you understand. There's only one Ryan Dean, as far as I am concerned. But it would be nice to bring back some of his traditions. The football matches, especially the ones he would throw together on Thanksgiving. Thirty, forty people on each side. It used to make the local paper! That's what I remember. And that's what I'd love to see again.

"Maybe someday, way in the future, I'll have my own kids and we'll start our own traditions. I'll tell them about their grandpa..."

He trailed off and stared into the fire.

Teddy reached across and patted him on the head.

"Elliana?" he said. "Do you think you'll end up travelling when you get home?"

"I'm not sure," she replied. "I probably will at some point. But the world is always going to be there and I'm having fun where I am. It's nice. It's like you said, Jack, about what you've been doing all along. I suppose the main thing is to be happy. In whatever you're doing. I was happy yesterday, I will be happy when I'm back home..."

"What about Louise? Do you think you'll meet up with her again?"

Elliana thought for a while.

"I honestly don't know. It's not my decision to make really. I'll leave it up to fate or destiny. I loved meeting her and I love her for what she did for me – I'll never forget it. The thing is... There's a lot of Louises out there in the world that I can have so much fun with. But there's so many more Ellianas back at home, too scared to take that first step out of their door, waiting on their own little saviour.

"Maybe I can be that person for someone. Someday."

"I'm sure wherever Louise is, she'd be proud of you," said Teddy and Elliana smiled.

"And what about you then?" she asked Teddy. "Do you know what you'll do with yourself?"

Teddy sat back and exhaled. "Well, like I said before, I love what I do. I love helping people find the answers they seek. Even today, it was lovely being able to chat so openly with all of you. I think you are all fascinating, magnificent people and if I ever meet anyone in the real world half as good as any of you, then I will be a very lucky man."

"What about you, though?" asked Wes. "Will you be alright?"

"Yes," Teddy responded firmly. "I just need time to heal."

He smiled at everyone around the fire and looked up towards the sky. Time and friends. He had spent less than a day in the company of new friends and already most of the constant pain he had carried with him for so long floated above him into the air and disappeared beyond the trees, settling in the sky among the stars.

Underneath the canopy of gleaming starlight, the fire dwindled to its final embers. The time had been spent talking and laughing, not a worry given to the mysteries of the foreign land the travellers found themselves in. Each giggle and every chuckle was in stark contrast to the foreboding aura of the eerie wasteland. Every smile was a beacon of warmth that repelled the sinister chill as it gathered close to their hearts.

The fire spat quietly, a dull yellow flame dancing on the wood.

"I'm pretty tired now, I think I might try for some sleep," said Jack.

Lesley yawned widely.

"Could be another long, hard day tomorrow," commented Wes.

"Let's hope not," said Teddy. "Let's just hope we get home."

"Alright," said Lesley sluggishly. "I guess it's goodnight everyone."

The final flame on the fire fizzled into smoke and drifted upwards in a slow, steady stream.

"Sweet dreams," said Elliana.

Epilogue

The clouds hung high in the sky the day Teddy awoke from the dream. He opened his eyes slowly and found himself sitting on the worn-down couch in his office. Outside the window was an unspectacular splash of grey, an unimpressive smattering of clouds, wind, and rain.
Teddy stood up and walked towards the window. Lost in hazy memories of deserts and roads, he smiled to himself.

*

Lesley opened her eyes as if for the first time. Her desk was as cluttered as always. It was no wonder she knocked that picture off...
She hesitated. The picture frame? That seemed a lifetime ago.

On the floor there were small fragments of glass and there, just beyond reach, was the photograph of her mother and father, taken all those years ago. Carefully, she picked it up and placed it back on the desk, brushing the glass off. She set it next to the other picture she kept there: it was an old photo of Lesley and her first ever group of friends – the children from the orphanage. Lesley was standing at the edge, slightly apart from the other children but holding the hand of one of the adults. She smiled happily at the kind face of Maria.

Lesley sat back in her chair. After several minutes she leaned over and picked up the phone.

*

"Son?" called a voice from a great distance.

Wes opened his eyes. He was sitting on the porch steps, looking out over his parents' front garden - the old brown fence, split in places, and the overgrown grass, edging onto the path. Beyond the garden was the long road into town, starting at the gate and pulling all the way towards the horizon.

"Son?" called the voice again, this time from behind him. "Did you fall asleep?"

Wes turned around. He looked up into the face of his mother. He smiled widely, leapt to his feet and hugged her tight.

His mother laughed in surprise. "Wes!" she smiled. "What are you doing home? Are you back for Thanksgiving?"

Wes hesitated.

"Thanks... Thanksgiving?"

He turned his head around and saw the old farmer's field out of the corner of his eye.

"Of course I'm home for Thanksgiving, ma! And I have a brilliant idea..."

*

"Ellie?"

Elliana awoke on a comfortable bed of pillows. She recognised her friend's voice. Where was she?

"Elliana!" Rachel called. "I've only been gone five minutes, how did you fall asleep?"

"I... I don't know, that was weird."

"Are they overworking you at that call centre? I don't know why you're still there."

Elliana stretched and yawned.

"The people are fun," she replied. "Besides, I'm thinking of quitting soon anyway."

"Really?" Rachel asked. "Haven't you been saying that for two years now?"

"Yes, I suppose I have but I've got everything I need now. And it's time I did something different."

"What, career-wise? Or are you thinking – *again* – of going abroad?"

"I don't know yet. Another country sounds good. Do you want to come?"

Rachel hesitated and fidgeted with her hands. "I dunno, I haven't saved up a lot of money and... Shouldn't we really make a plan for it?"

Elliana smiled mischievously.

*

Not for the first time in his life, Jack felt the full force of a football smack him in the face. It jolted him into consciousness.

"Wha--" he groaned.

Blinking rapidly, his eyes watering, he searched for the culprit. In front of him stood a small boy wearing the light blue of Manchester City.

"I'm sorry!" the boy yelled.

"What the-- Why would you kick a ball at me? Is it because I play for United?"

"No, no!" the boy said. "I tried to get you to header it but it slipped from my hands! I wouldn't hurt you, you're my favourite player!"

Jack laughed groggily then stumbled to his feet.

"Hey, don't worry about it, kid, but I'm going to have to score against your team for that one!"

He fumbled in his pocket for his phone, punched a few buttons, and pressed it to his ear.

"Jack!"

"Hey, Marco, I'm coming over in about half an hour, is that alright?"

"Yeah, cool, what's up?"

"Well, I sort of had this idea. I was thinking about setting up a centre for kids in the community... but then a five year old City fan just kicked a ball at my face so I might be reconsidering..."

"Haha, really? Sounds interesting. You heading straight round?"

"Yeah, I won't be long. Oh, yeah, and I just had the weirdest dream..."

Acknowledgements

I don't make a habit of hiding the person I am.
Therefore, the people who deserve my gratitude for
everything they have done for me do not need to see
their name in print to know it is appreciated.

Every person I have ever met has, in some way,
helped to make me the person I am today. For your
time, I thank you.

I reserve special thanks for you, the reader, for
immersing yourself in these pages.
I don't have the words to describe my eternal
appreciation.

Legal/Copyright

Printed in Great Britain
by Amazon